My Headless Son Fred And His Head Baby Brother Headley

T. Hudson Roberts

ArrowGate

Published by Arrow Gate Publishing Ltd 2020

15 14 13 12 11 10 9 8 7 6

A CIP catalogue record for this book is available from the British Library.
ISBN 978-1-913142-18-6

Arrow Gate Publishing 85, Great Portland Street, London W1W 7LT

For my sister Les, who supports all my creative ideas and maybe one or two of my non-creative ideas.

Everything

FAMILY IS EVERYTHING. That was what my grandfather, Filmon, whom I was named after, had once told me when I was six years old. I wasn't sure if he had mentioned it to his son, my father, who'd escaped responsibility to an unknown location, leaving a wife and two boys in a struggling household.

If I ever have two boys, I will never leave them, my heart and mind harmonised.

Family is everything.

In a sour mood, I grumbled all the way home from a tense day at work. A few of my co-workers had been on my case, envious of my promotion to Wildlife Waste Handler, at a prominent national park. Previously, I'd held an assistant-supervisory position in the Beaver

Creek Sanitation Department, located inside a three-story office building. But now my duties took me outdoors in the sweet, fresh air, among frolicking animals and under a vast, picturesque sky. Jealousy had always seemed to percolate with my co-workers whenever I'd moved up the ladder of opportunity.

It was Halloween night, and there I was finally at home, sitting on my leather recliner, eating a gourmet microwave dinner, and watching my favourite reality TV show, The Bachelor. I made sure to turn off all the lights in the house because once again I had forgotten it was Halloween and hadn't bought any candy.

"I hope the neighbourhood brats will get the hint and don't come ringin' my doorbell," I muttered to myself, still feeling a bit irritable.

"Ding Dong!

"*Dammit!*" I swore under my breath.

Two eight-year-old twin boys dressed up as Batman and Robin stood tiptoed, pushing their faces up against the glass portion of my front door.

"Trick or treat, Mr Trout! We see you in there!" the little Batman shouted.

I scooted further down in the recliner and mumbled, "Clueless kids. Don't they know when the lights are out, people are out."

"Come onnnn...Mr Trout, open up! Don't be a cheap bastard againnnn...this year!" screamed the little Batman brat in a dragging, blistering tone.

"Yeah, we saw you duck down!" the Robin twin added. I shook my head in frustration and exhaled, "Geesh...I gotta get the hell outta here."

A moment after the twins had left, I slipped through the rear door of my house and hopped over a dog-eared wooden fence that separated my backyard and a narrow alley. When I dropped down onto the alley street, an annoying sigh flushed out of me when I eyed the Caped Crusader twins and two other costumed midgets at the alley's west entrance.

I closed my eyes and froze, hoping they wouldn't see me in the murky darkness. Unfortunately, I was standing under a high-powered night-light exposing me like I was the lead in a Broadway show.

"Hey, there's Mr Trout!" a squeaky voice yelled.

"Let's get that cheap bastard!" another bratty voice screeched.

"Yeah!" Chorused the other two high-pitched hooligans.

I stretched out an eyelid and muscled an eyeball to the side, shocked to see four preteen brats heading my way, seemingly with mob mentalities. "Dammit!" I was pretty sure I could kick one eight-year-old's ass. But four? I ran off like an Olympic sprinter.

Although I couldn't kick all of their asses, I was positive I could outrun them—I had been the second alternate on my junior varsity track team. It wasn't long before I put enough distance between us that they soon quit, flashing me several farewell middle fingers. I then turned around and raised my arms in triumph.

"Ha! Losers! I still got my speed, baby! Beavercreek Junior High in the house!"

After I celebrated my victory, the contents of my dinner gushed out of me and onto the sidewalk. Three long breaths later, my dizziness and exhaustion faded, and I found myself across the street from the local cemetery called Mac and Donald's Burial World, owned by two brothers who'd lost a lawsuit for placing two large golden arches at the entrance. Now there was just one ash-grey arch. Suddenly I heard a strange noise coming from the outer edge of the cemetery. It sounded like a woman moaning as if she was bumping the nasty dance. Surely it was my duty as a concerned citizen to investigate.

I used soft steps, activating the peeping Tom...I mean...investigator in me, toward the area where I'd heard the sound. Under celestial lights, the cemetery glowed an indigo hue, which allowed me to see my way through the dark backdrop of Red Cedar trees. It was quite creepy to be in a cemetery at night, but my horniness tends to override budding fear shamelessly. I suddenly cringed from a cool, stiff breeze that slapped at the back of my sweaty t-shirt, which pushed into my skin, giving me a sharp, uncomfortable tingling sensation, and regret entering the cemetery in the first place.

I soon reached a large patch of grass, in which an open grave lay in between two enclosed gravesites. There in the semi-darkness, I was suddenly startled by a fully clothed woman climbing out of the six-foot deep hole. When she appeared with her clothes on, I was more disappointed than startled. My expectations weren't always what I'd expected.

"Excuse me, Miss. Are you all right?" I asked. My voice was calming.

She seemed spiritless but managed to nod back at me. She then leaned back on a small mound of dirt as her feet dangled from the upper edge of the grave.

I crept toward her in an unthreatening manner, hunched over. Then I peeked down into the grave and saw that it was empty.

"Do you want me to help you up?"

Without a word, she nodded again.

"Okay, up we go," I said, placing both of my hands under her arms and gently raising her.

As I escorted the young woman out of the cemetery and onto the sidewalk, I couldn't help but notice how cold her arms and hands were. But she wasn't shivering. Also, she was drifting beside me in a dreamy state, almost lifeless as though she was sleepwalking.

I became worried and halted our steps and asked her where she lived. She turned around and pointed a wilted finger back at the cemetery.

I scrunched up my face. "You mean...you were sleeping in the grave?"

The young woman looked embarrassed, slightly shrugging her shoulders and nodding.

I wondered if she was a homeless mute. "Can you speak?"

She hit me with another nod. Yet this time she opened her mouth and struggled for words, "Ye...Yes. I—

"What's your name?"

"Mil...Mildead. Mildead Pierce."

"Mildred?"

She shook her head. "Mildead."

"Mil...dead?" I repeated.

She gave me one big nod. Poor thing...can't pronounce her R's, I thought to myself.

"My name is Filmon Trout. Now listen, Mildead, you can't go back to that grave. It's not safe for a young lady to be out alone, late at night...especially in a cemetery.

Would you like to stay at my place for a while? I have an extra room."

She grinned and said, "Yes, of course. I would love to stay at your place. Thank you, Filmon."

I snapped my head back, and half smiled, shocked from her sudden burst of connecting words.

We strolled along arm in arm like a longtime couple in love. I had to admit it felt good to hold a woman again and it didn't matter that we'd just met. It had been quite a while since I'd been with a woman—4 years, ten months, and 24 days give or take a few hours. I wasn't sure why it had been so long since I'd dated a female. I wasn't shy and approaching women wasn't a problem for me. Although it was possible my rap game needed work, so maybe my brother Zeke's suggestion of *hi, will you have sex with me?* Hadn't been a good pick-up line after all.

I've always thought I had this coolness that women lusted for, and the ladies surely loved thin men who wore eyeglasses. Well, that was what my mother, bless her soul, had passed on to me when we had the "sex talk" on my thirtieth birthday; maybe women didn't get my complexity.

Anyway, Mildred...I mean Mil-dead—a cute girl, didn't appear to mind that I was holding her firmly, and she seemed to like me, so I thought.

Once Mildead and I arrived at my house, an avocado-green two-storey stucco, I insisted that she take a shower. She stank like a dead antelope. Of course, I hadn't said she stank. My mother had raised me to be tactful. I had commented that she didn't smell like anything living on this earth. *Cleanliness is next to goblins' nests*, my mother had often said. But before Mildead took a shower, I had given her a few of my mother's sleepwear and un-dergarments: a silk nightgown; long-line bra; a nylon half-slip; and a thong. My mother had always loved to mix past and modern fashions.

When Mildead emerged from the shower, I noticed how pale she was—as shades of green and light-blue blended ...sort of sickly, and her basalt-coloured eyes—tired and bloodshot. I promptly showed her to the guest room and sat her down on a queen-size bed. While Mildead looked ill, she sure didn't act like it. My new friend was a bit playful, checking me out from head to toe, licking her lips as if I was a piece of prime rib.

"Mildead, are you...horny?" I guessed and hoping she appreciated my naughty talk.

She shook her head and replied, "I'm hungry."

Elusive. A saucy expression bloomed on my face.

"Are you hungry for me?"

Her eyes widened, nearly popping out of her head. "Yes, hungry for you!" She came to me like a vampire in heat, knocking me down to the floor. Next thing I knew, she was on top of me.

"Easy, girl. There's enough of me to—Aieeeee!" I screamed after she bit me on the hand. "Mil-dead, I'm not into that rough stuff!" I stretched out my arms to keep her at bay. "I'm delicate!" I managed to push her off me and sprang up on my feet. She countered with her own athletic maneuver to be upright, using a wrestling kick-up from the floor. I then reversed my steps away from her, but she kept creeping toward me.

"I'm hungry for you, Filmon," uttered Mildead, snapping her teeth.

"I'm hungry for you, too. But maybe we can leave out the biting..."

I backed out of the bedroom while she kept following me with dog-hungry eyes. I wasn't scared, just a bit confused—I never had a woman who was horny for me. Next, I felt the wooden bannister at the top of the staircase rubbing against my lower back. I then backpedaled down a couple of steps, all the while getting a bit horny myself. I decided to stop, allowing her to catch me. But before I made my sexy move, the combination of jerking my head back and dancing the Running Man, Mildead tripped on her own foot and tumbled forward. I frantically reached out to get a hold of her, but she slipped from my grasp and toppled over my shoulder, taking me with her down the staircase. Dammit!

I woke a moment later in a swirling daze at the bottom of the stairs, stretched out on my back. When my mind cleared, I began to warily move different parts of my body, hoping nothing was broken. Relief soon enveloped me after I realised there was nothing more than an ache on my bum. I managed to raise my head and was shocked to see Mildead on her knees, picking up her teeth, one by one from off the floor.

"Mildead, are you okay?"

She turned to me, expressing a wide, toothless grin. Shock then hit me hard.

"Mildead, you have no teeth!"

That instant, she opened both of her hands and showed me practically every single tooth that was once in her mouth—incisors; canines; molars; even a gold tooth. Apparently, she had landed face-first on the bottom step, for there was a three-inch chip in the wood. I picked myself up from the floor and raised Mildead to a standing position. It was odd, and she didn't seem hurt at all; it was like nothing had happened.

"How 'bout you? Are you otay, Hilmon?" Mildead asked.

"Huh?" It was difficult to grasp her current toothless language.

"Are you otay?"

"Oh, yeah. I...I'm okay. I'm just worried about you." She smiled. "Dun werwee, I heel hine."

She may have said, don't worry, I feel fine. Or, don't worry, high heels are mine. I believed it was the former.

Mildead was indeed a tough woman, and I was turned on by that; I loved the fact that she was resilient. Yet, she now sported a granny smile, with that dark, cavernous mouth of hers, which I certainly didn't mind one bit. I proceeded to put my arm around her waist and guided her upstairs to the guest room. I promptly laid her down on the bed and kissed her on the cheek. But before I turned to leave, she patted the bed, motioning for me to join her.

Excitement jump-started my loins, and I leapt up and belly-flopped on the bed, crashing down next to her. Without hesitation, I attacked her with kisses. She retaliated by gumming my neck.

"Hey, that tickles," I said, giggling.

Soon after the giggling and gumming, we began to make love, stirring up passion and emotion—two things I never thought I had. Mildead was indeed a greedy gummer. It was probably a new thing that women did these days; I even started to gum her, but I just folded my lips. Other than sloppy kisses, the only negative about our sexy time was that her skin was cold to the touch.

Although I didn't mind it much since my body was overheated anyway, balancing things out.

It was a good Halloween.

My Boys Arrive!

SEVERAL MONTHS HAD PASSED since Mildead and I had met on Halloween night. I was definitely in love, and I was sure Mildead felt the same way about me. She hadn't left me yet, so that may have been an indicator that love was between us. Mildead was now the only woman in my life since my mother had left me the day after my thirtieth birthday to fend for myself from the overwhelming reality of the world. Not five minutes after she'd left, my mother was hit by a speeding ice cream truck, as she had crossed the street, dying instantly. I was so glad we had the "sex talk" before she'd passed away; it had been constructive on Halloween night.

But during our short relationship, Mildead was acting strangely. Once or twice a week, she would go out late at night while I was asleep. I'd caught her one early morning at 3 am, returning to the house.

I then asked her where she had gone, but she'd only shrugged her shoulders without saying anything. I didn't want to press her about it and have her think I was clingy. There were also strange occurrences going on in the household and neighbourhood. First, my two hamsters, Timmy and Jimmy, went missing, then my cat Charlie disappeared. I was heartbroken; it was like losing my children.

In the neighbourhood, two of the neighbours down the block had said their dogs were missing. Besides, Mary, my elderly next-door neighbour, had mentioned that her son, who was out on parole from prison, had never shown up for his welcome home party. Last weekend, my neighbours and I had held a meeting at my house to discuss the disappearances of Mary's son and the animals. At that meeting, I had boldly stepped up to the plate and nominated myself to lead the Neighbourhood Watch Program, since I'd taken a criminology class back in junior college.

My neighbours and I soon concluded that there must have been a serial kidnapper in our midst—a kidnapper who held no distinction between animal or man. A few days ago, we held a press conference and reached out to the public for help. Mary had pleaded for the kidnapper to return her forty-two-year-old son. As for the two neighbours who had their dogs taken, both had stated clearly their heartrending pleas. Of course, I had to have my say in regards to Timmy, Jimmy and Charlie.

"Mr Kidnapper, if you can't return all three of my pets, or at least return my cat, Charlie. He's a rare breed and worth a lot of money. He also has a diamond-studded collar around his neck that's worth a small fortune, too. Thank you, Mr Kidnapper."

My first duty as acting chairman of the Neighbourhood Watch program was to appoint Mildead as graveyard supervisor, knowing that she would be out and about at that time anyway. Mildead was a tough and fearless girl who had fallen down a flight of stairs and slept in a cemetery. So I wasn't too worried about her.

**

It was a warm Sunday night, Mildead and I sat in the living room, watching a horror movie, My Momma's a Zombie. I barely kept my eyes open, and I was so scared. But Mildead kept cracking up throughout the entire flick and kept yelling, "Hake! Ho unhealiptic!" Since she had no teeth, it took me nearly an hour to get what she was saying: Fake! So unrealistic! I have never seen her so passionate. Whenever a horror film would come on the television, Mildead would get into it as though she was the lead actress. If a zombie movie would come on, forget about it; she loved anything zombie. And I'd even joked that she looked like a zombie. She'd just smiled and thanked me.

Later, while we both were in bed, I noticed her stomach protruded more than usual. I had first thought she'd been overeating. Then I realised that I have never seen her eat. She'd always gave the excuse that she wasn't hungry.

"Honey, your tummy is getting really big. I would say that you're overeating, but I never see you eat anything. I'm worried. It ...it may be a tumour or something," I said, rubbing her stomach.

"I ee...lay ah ny, why ur sleebing," she replied.

Geesh, I gotta get her some dentures, I thought. I was sure she had said, I eat ... late at night, while you're sleeping. I took that as a logical remark.

"Oh, okay. I just thought maybe—"

"Weer ha-ing ah ba-by."

"What! We're having a baby?"

Mildead nodded as a wide grin stretched her pale green face.

I jumped up from off the bed and raised my arms high in the air.

"Yes! I'm gonna be a father! I knew my little fishys could swim, baby!"

I broke into my sexy dance—head jerk, Running Man.

The day finally arrived when Mildead went into labour. I panicked. Practically everything I did was made in haste. When Mildead had said her water broke, I checked the water cooler for leaks. I had telephoned the hospital, but it was my cat Charlie's vet. When I had called a taxi, I soon realised I had a car. I then sped off in my 1978 AMC Pacer, on my way to the hospital; got two blocks; screeched a u-turn; and raced back home to pick up Mildead. She wasn't too happy about that. Eventually, we had made it to the hospital without the baby popping out.

Once we were in the hospital room, the medical staff did their thing. Their first action was to pick me up off the floor since I'd fainted from a panic attack. Luckily, there was an open bed next to Mildead so that I wouldn't be too far from her. After ten minutes of blacking out, I woke up to find a doctor and a nurse standing over a spread-eagled Mildead who was ready to receive our baby. As soon as I propped myself up to a sitting position, the female doctor motioned for me to join her. I shook my head and mouthed a silent "no way."

But Mildead gave me the evil eye and a snapping head jerk. A fraction of a second later, I stood at the foot of

Mildead's hospital bed, staring open-jawed at her birth canal. I felt another fainting spell coming on.

"Here it comes. I think I see the head," the doctor announced.

I bent over and braced myself, placing one hand on the end corner of the bed and my other hand on the doctor's lab coat, nearly yanking it off her back.

The doctor turned to me, donning an annoyed look on her face.

"Mr Trout, stop pulling my—"

"Oh, sorry, doc," I said, releasing her coat.

I took my eyes away from the action spot and looked at Mildead; she was calm and collected. I'd seen films and had heard stories of women in pain, straining to give birth. But my brave and strong Mildead had a look of serenity like she was knitting a sweater. I was dumbfounded, yet at the same time proud of her, and by just seeing how calm she was, I felt better.

Then it happened.

Screams filled the room.

"What's the mat—" Shock slammed into me so hard that I had trouble breathing. I couldn't believe what I was seeing.

"Where's my baby's head!"

The doctor had a blank expression on her face, holding the infant in her cupped hands. "I...I cannot explain this. Your baby is alive and kicking, yet he has no head."

"He?" asked Mildead, smiling and seemingly unfazed by the shocking turn of events.

The doctor returned a slight nod, still in a state of disbelief. "Ye...yes. It's a boy."

Mildead sat upright and stretched out her arms. "Yay! Le me ho him!"

The doctor tightened her forehead.

"Excuse me?"

"Let her hold the baby," I explained, not realising that I was getting better at understanding Mildead's toothless language.

Mildead handled our baby with caution and care. She seemed dazzled by the infant's vitality, and she didn't appear to mind that our son didn't have a head. Mildead put me at ease by the way she expressed her motherly love to our baby. So what if the kid didn't have a head. As long as he was healthy and still kicking, he would be our son forever. At least he had a little winky—it would be tough for a male child to go through life without one.

I slipped around the corner of the bed and placed myself at Mildead's side. It warmed my heart to see Mildead and our newborn son together. Gently, I touched the baby's toes and fingers, then I counted each digit, just to make sure they were all there. I gazed at my son's tiny body, nervous but full of joy. It was the first time I had ever been near an infant.

My son was beautiful, wrinkly and reddish-brown. His brown skin had to be attributed to Native American blood from my mother's great-great grand-uncle's second cousin who had received a blood transfusion from a gay Chinese railroad worker who was half Apache. My heart soon began to sigh as the thought of my brown-skinned ancestors lingered gaily in my mind. I then noticed an oval-shaped bald spot in between the baby's shoulders, where his head would've been if he had one. And near his right nipple was a small birthmark, the shape of an arch, just like the one in front of his mother's previous address. Life was sure full of ironies.

Mildead lifted her eyes off the baby and gestured with a head nod for me to hold him. I hesitated, for I was afraid I'd drop the little fellow on the floor, I was so nervous. I put out my hands and received my son from Mildead, who eyed the baby carefully. My heart melted as I gently rocked my son, who gradually fell asleep.

"Hilmon, nay him," Mildead uttered in her toothless language.

"Name him?"

Mildead returned a slight nod.

I was so honoured that my eyes welled up with tears. I peered down at my son and slipped into deep thought.

"Hmm...all righty. How about...um...Randolph?"

Mildead wrinkled her nose and shook her head.

"No, huh?" More deep thought. "Um...Milton?"

Another nose wrinkle.

"Festor?"

Mildead's head shook wildly.

"Barabbas?"

Mildead spat on the floor, and then she gave me the Finger.

"All right, all right, I give up. You name him," I said frustratedly.

It was Mildead's turn to be in deep thought until her eyes widened.

"Red."

"Huh? Red?"

Mildead tried harder, struggling with her toothless language.

"No. Bred!"

I scratched my head while still holding my son. "Bread?"

She spat on the floor again.

"Pred!"

I finally got it.

"Oh, Fred!" I really gotta get her some dentures, I thought.

Mildead sighed in relief and nodded.

"Fred, huh?" Another deep-thought moment. "Hmm...Fred...with no head... I like it!"

After Mildead and I mouthed off our son's new name at him a dozen times as he was sleeping, a team of doctors, including the hospital's director, barged in the room to examine him. They surrounded Mildead's bed and were in awe and shock when they set their eyes upon the baby. Then all of a sudden, Fred involuntarily moved his arms and legs while still sleeping. Every single onlooking doctor gasped in disbelief—never had anyone seen a live, headless baby.

The doctors huddled together and started to whisper among themselves. I didn't have a good feeling. It was never good when people would whisper behind your back, especially if they were doctors. I looked to Mildead who caught on to my uneasy bearing. Then she began to feel a bit uncomfortable herself. Our internal discomfort was indeed warranted when the doctors broke out of their huddle, wearing obvious fake smiles.

"Mr and Mrs Trout, your baby boy is a medical miracle. Never in my years in the medical field, have I seen anything like this? Your baby defies the laws of human biology. He shouldn't be alive," the hospital director said, teeming with wonderment. "I must insist that we keep your baby here for further physical and mental evaluations. Well, maybe not mental...."

Mildead stretched out and snatched Fred from my arms, holding him firmly.

"No. Ow ob dakweshun!"

The director sent Mildead a bewildered look and redirected it to me.

I thought for a moment and replied, "She either said no, I'm an equestrian. Or no, out of the question. I think it was the latter, Doc."

The director turned back to Mildead. "But, Mrs Trout. We must find out why your baby is—"

"No. An, I'm nah a mishes. I hab no ree un my binger," answered Mildead. Then she gave me an exhausted slanted eye.

The hospital director turned to me again.

For some typical male reason, I got that one right away. Reluctantly, I repeated Mildead's answer in the English language, "No. And, I'm not a Mrs I have no ring on my finger."

"Oh!" a few of the doctors crooned, spouting off at the same time.

The hospital director frowned. He was a little fellow with a receding hairline that nearly ebbed back to the top of his head. And he seemed to be one of those guys who had battled being short all of his life, becoming an over-bearing bully of a man who had always gotten his way.

"Please, Mrs...Miss...we need to evaluate your baby to see if he's healthy enough to go home," pleaded the director.

Mildead stood up from the bed, holding Fred in her arms and shouted, "No! No! No!" She then flipped him off with a sturdy middle finger. Ire singed at the hospital director's ego. He called for another huddle and whispered to the other doctors, discussing their next move while Mildead and I did our own whispering.

I leaned in close to Mildead, our heads nearly touching. "What? You wanna get outta here? Are you sure, honey?"

Mildead nodded before she raced toward the door, carrying our son. I then flung myself forward and followed, covering Mildead's rear as her pale butt exposed itself out from the flapping hospital gown. I kept trying to close her gown flaps as I ran—no one was going to see my girl's ass but me.

We made a sharp right out of Mildead's room and headed for the elevators. I cut short my duty as Mildead's butt coverer and moved ahead of her to push the elevator button. I kept pushing the button to speed up the elevator since I'd seen people do it before. Shoot, it must be broke, I thought. I pounded the closed elevator door and cursed its speed mechanism. Then both Mildead and I whirled around and saw the doctors trotting toward us as the elevator doors finally slid open. In an instant, we were inside the elevator, watching the doors close on the doctors who were a second too late to nab us. Haha!

Within a blink of an eye, the elevator doors opened again, and the doctors were standing in front of us. I forgot to push the lobby button.

"Dammit!"

In an authoritative tone, the hospital director ordered, "Please, step out of the elevator and come with us."

Mildead and I walked out of the elevator, with our heads down, our escape thwarted. The director led us along the   fourth-floor corridor, and then two male nurses joined the procession of doctors who were at our rear. A security guard and a female nurse also followed as word spread rapidly of a headless baby. There were so many people that soon gathered around us, and I felt like we were in a civil rights march. All of a sudden, Mildead held up her steps, causing a human domino effect, as doctors bumped into one another.

"Mildead, what's wrong?" I asked sharply.

Mildead stretched out her arms and showed Fred to me.

"What the heck!"

Loud gasps exploded behind us.

A tiny foot was sticking out from between the baby's shoulders.

"Fred's gotta foot head!" I shouted frantically.

In less than a minute, practically the whole hospital staff gathered around us to witness the phenomenon.

"Hey, now a leg is showing!" one of the male nurses cried out.

"Back up! Everyone, back up!" yelled the director. "Let me take a look at...what in the mother of freaks is that!"

A baby's leg began to ease out from the top centre of Fred's torso. Then another leg. The bottom half of a male infant appeared next. As another baby was pushing itself out of my son, Fred's arms and legs flailed wildly. It only took a moment for the metamorphosis to complete. A live, fully developed infant materialised before our eyes, with its head conjoined between Fred's shoulders while its body dangled in the air. It seemed like the infant was relaxing on its side, lounging atop of Fred's torso.

I was in shock once again.

"Mildead... It...it looks like Fred has a head, but it's not his. The scene was eerie, but then it quickly turned magical. "Honey, Fred has a twin brother!"

Mildead expressed the widest of grins and bent her head to kiss both babies.

After calming himself with scientific reasoning, the hospital director said, "Mr Trout, now we must examine these babies."

I glanced at Mildead, whose eyes and mouth screamed, "No!"

With everyone gawking at my newborn sons, I espied a door with an exit sign over it. That must be the stairwell, I said to myself. I looked to Mildead again and gestured with a head nod toward the exit. She nodded back, getting my drift.

"Look, it's the king of England!" I shouted, pointing behind the crowd of medical staff.

I wasn't sure if there was a king of England, but every single head turned around and fell for my bluff or semi-bluff. Mildead snapped to attention, catching on to my ruse, and she took off running for the exit. I followed close behind, trying my best to keep up. Once again, I kept my girl's butt from showing through her hospital gown by using keener blocking tactics.

We scampered down four flights of stairs, inside a hollow and windowless stairwell. I thought I could run fast, but Mildead skipped every other step, even with the twins in her arms. She was really booking. The sound of voices and tramping of feet were getting louder, so I didn't have to look back to know that several people were chasing us. Into the lobby we ran, dodging nurses, doctors, and patients in wheelchairs. Within a few heart-beats, we were out of the hospital, rushing toward my car, which was near the entrance, and sitting in a handi-capped parking space.

As our little family sat in the Pacer, relieved and heading for home, Mildead and I sang in harmony the theme from the Partridge Family, "Hello, world, here's a song that we're singin', c'mon be happy. A whole lotta lovin' is what we'll be bringin', we'll make you happy...."

CHAPTER 3

My Boys are Baby Geniuses

WHEN MILDEAD AND I arrived home, we began thinking up names for our youngest son. It was more difficult than we thought it would be. Throughout the night, we tossed random names at each other to no avail. The next day, I decided to call my good friend and co-worker Janet, to help us out. Janet was a professional baby namer—she had five kids, naming them all. When I'd asked her on the phone if she could be the godmother of our baby boys, she'd teared up all through our conversation, hung up, then came right over. It was the first time that anyone had asked her to be a godmother; therefore, she was truly honoured. So were we.

Janet Easley appeared at the front door of my home, projecting a massive smile on her face. I hugged her as soon as she stepped into the house. She was in her late forties, yet she had a youthful look to her, especially of one who was a mother of five adult children. A tall and voluptuous woman, heavy on the top, heavier on the bottom, Janet carried her size and weight well. She was nearly three hundred pounds, and yet her weight never seemed to be an issue with her—athleticism and big bones ran in her family. Janet was also the kindest person I've ever known; she would be an ideal godmother.

I led her into the living room and offered her a seat on the sofa.

"Filmon, where's Mildead?" Janet asked.

"Oh, she's upstairs. She'll be down with the boys in a minute." I sat on my recliner and kicked out the footrest.

"I see that you still have the plastic on this sofa," said Janet, smiling.

"Yeah, it's a reminder of my mother."

"Filmon James Trout, this sofa's older than you are. Why don't you just get a new one?"

"Um...I kinda like it. My mother—"

"Oh, hello, my dear!" greeted Janet, as Mildead entered the living room, carrying the babies.

Mildead returned the greeting, "Helyo, Ja-et!"

Janet rose from the sofa and spread her arms to welcome Mildead and the boys.

"Congratulations!" Janet kissed Mildead on both cheeks. "Let's see my two godsons."

Mildead tilted and raised her folded arms to give Janet a better look at the twins.

"Oh, Mildead, he's so adorable. Is this Fred or the one I'm going to name?"

"He's the one you're gonna name," I replied in haste, so I wouldn't have to repeat Mildead's in-evitable jumbled answer.

Janet turned a curious profile. "Oh, okay. Then where's Fred?"

Mildead pulled down the rest of the blanket that was covering Fred, who was moving his little arms like he was swimming the breaststroke. Mildead then gasped an open-jaw expression when Janet's body went limp.

Janet awoke on the floor just as I was giving her mouth-to-mouth resuscitation.

"Yes! You're alive!" I cried out, relieved.

Janet heaved herself up to a sitting position and whined, "Ew! What were you doing?"

"I was bringing you back to life with CPR," I explained, looking serious.

Janet twisted her mouth.

"I'm pretty sure you weren't supposed to use your tongue, Filmon."

"Oh...sorry. It was my first time. I thought you had a heart attack."

"I think I just fainted from..."

"From what?"

"I...I was just caught off guard by your babies. Th...there are two babies, right?"

I presented my friend with an assuring smile and replied.

"Of course. Fred just doesn't have a head. But I believe he's a healthy all-American boy. Now his younger brother has his head attached between Fred's shoulders—siamese-like. Do you follow me?"

Janet had a befuddled expression on her face. "Yeah. But how is Fred still functioning without a head?"

I shrugged my shoulders.

"I really don't know. The doctors don't even know. They said it was a medical miracle. Anyway, are you ready to name Fred's younger brother?"

Janet smiled.

"Sure."

"Great. You're one in a million, Janet."

Janet rose to her feet unassisted, refusing my help—a feat in itself for a three-hundred pounder.

Then, she sat herself back down on the sofa, next to Mildead, who was still holding the babies. Janet leaned over and set her eyes on the twin boys once again, this time prepared.

"Can I hold them?"

Mildead smiled and offered her sons to Janet.

Janet kissed Fred's shoulder, and then she kissed his little brother on the forehead. She tilted her head and paused to think up an appropriate name for Fred's twin. After a quiet moment, Janet broke the silence, "Before I came, I already had a couple of names in mind. But I'm not going to use them. Instead, since Fred doesn't have a head...sorry, I didn't mean to rhyme. I'm going to name his baby brother, Headley."

Mildead and I caught each other's wide-eyed gaze, and we both nodded in agreement.

"Janet, that's a perfect name!"

I felt like she'd invented the wheel. "My boy, Headley... I love it!"

Mildead clapped.

"I wuv id, too!"

Janet expressed a stretching grin. She didn't have any problem understanding Mildead.

Mildead then let out a long sigh of joy.

"Pred an Headry!"

My grin matched Janet's. "That's our boys!"

The stream glistened in the sunlight, flowing with much determination through the rocky terrain at the southern edge of Kuruk National Park. Kuruk, an Apache word for bear, was a fitting name for this particular verdant landmass which was teeming with various types of bears roaming its surroundings.

I was at the end of my shift, carefully examining the fresh bear droppings that were several yards away from the stream's bank. My job was to confiscate the waste for disposal before the rains washed it into the stream, contaminating the pristine waters. A duty I had ingeniously thought up on my own.

With my expertly trained eye for animal waste, I easily determined that it came from a male adult grizzly bear, due to the remains of roots and tubers in the faeces. What also helped in my assessment was that a male grizzly as big as a mountain, hovered over me on his hind legs as I was hunched over, sifting through his crap.

"Dammit!" Fear struck me in the heart while my whole body trembled.

At that moment, I felt I was going to be grizzly fodder and future bear crap.

My expertise in wildlife waste handling didn't prepare me for a confrontation with a massive grizzly bear who was either angry that I was in his territory or confused by my interest in his poop. I hoped it was the latter.

In slow motion, I curled up in a ball, all the while praying I wouldn't entice the bear to chew up my flesh as I moved.

"Please, don't eat me, Mr bear. Please...please..." I chanted under my breath. Then, with all the nerves twitching in my body from fright, I pooped in my pants. Not a defensive mechanism that I was hoping for.

The grizzly dropped to all fours, his front legs thumping on the ground. My eyes were shut, but I could smell the bear's odour, a cross between excrement and dirty laundry. Wait a minute, that was my smell...never mind. The grizzly nudged me with his broad snout, causing me to roll backward. After a few more rolls, I finally came to a stop in the same curled-up position with my eyes still closed, but I was nearer to the edge of the bank.

I continued my chanting.

"Please, don't eat me, Mr bear. Please, don't eat me, Mr bear..."

Something odd happened next. I felt the grizzly bear sniffing at my butt. Maybe he wanted to see why I'd been sniffing around his crap, by sniffing mine. When the grizzly had inhaled enough of my backside, he nudged me hard once more with his snout, and downward I tumbled off the bank, splashing down into the stream.

"Dammit!"

A quarter of a mile downstream, a park ranger fished me out of the water, then he reprimanded me for taking a dip during working hours. I would've told him the truth about the grizzly bear pushing me into the stream, but I kept mum for fear of constant ragging from coworkers. I was sure he would've ratted me out to them. My position as a Waste Handler was underappreciated in some circles, especially within the park ranger cast who were a pretentious lot. I was glad I'd failed the park ranger test five times, or I'd never been blessed with my current job position.

The traffic on the way home from work was ridiculous, backed up for miles. I was sitting in my car, bumper to bumper for 45 minutes. Usually, it would've taken me only 25 minutes to get home.

During that idle time in traffic, I thought about Fred and Headley. I couldn't wait to hold them in my arms. Play with them. Make them laugh. Sing to them. They were my inspiration, instilling my life with meaning and purpose. Vigour and joy sang throughout my household, stirring about in the form of my two beautiful boys.

I finally arrived at the house, hungry and exhausted, yet I had just enough energy left over to play with my kids. I opened the front door in an unintentionally rough manner like I was entering a saloon in the old west, and at the same time, I called out for my boys.

"Fred! Headley! Daddy's home!"

I held up my steps. In the living room were two strange women sitting on my sofa. Both women had that same pale, light-green complexion as Mildead. One woman had a nurse's outfit on, and the other was wearing outdated, bell-bottom blue jeans and a tie-dye, rainbow-coloured halter top. I cleared my throat before I introduced myself.

"Hello, ladies. I'm Filmon. And you are?"

The two women eyed me hard, checking me out from head to toe. The woman in the hippie outfit answered first in a monotone voice.

"Hello. We are Mildead's sisters. I'm Toodead. And this here is Sodead."

Her introduction caught me by surprise. "Mildead's sisters? But...Mildead had told me her two sisters had died."

Toodead and Sodead turned to each other and smirked.

"Oh, Mildead has always been a little fibber," Toodead replied.

"Who iz a pibber?" asked Mildead, just entering the living room from the kitchen, carrying Fred and Headley.

Confused, I blurted, "Mildead, I thought you said your sisters had died."

Mildead glanced at her sisters before she said, "Um...my udder two sisders die."

"Oh, okay. I thought you only had two sisters." Satisfied, I broke out in a smile. "Lemme see my boys."

Mildead gladly handed over Fred and Headley to me.

"Dang, they seem to have gotten bigger overnight... Hi, Fred. Hi, Headley." I shook Fred's hand and rubbed Headley's tummy.

"Daddy, that tickles," Headley said, giggling.

My face did a double-take.

"What in the son of Abraham was that!"

"Headry ka talk," explained Mildead.

"Talk? But how is that possible? He's only seven months old."

I gazed back at Headley, who showed me an innocent face with a curvy smile, showing pearly whites. "What! And he has nearly a full mouth of teeth! How can he talk and grow a bunch of teeth overnight?"

"Daddy, it sometimes happens with uber-intellectual children with fast growth hormones," mouthed Headley, using perfect enunciation.

"What the...fast growth hormones? I...I can't believe it...and uber? What's an uber?"

"You're funny, daddy."

Still, in disbelief, I asked.

"When did you learn how to speak?"

Headley showed off his teeth again and said, "Oh, just this morning."

I had to pinch myself on the top of my hand to be sure that I wasn't dreaming. I knew something was odd when I'd noticed the current size of my boys. In just seven months they have grown to a size of three-year-old toddlers, and a lot of that growth spurt came overnight. With Headley already talking clearly, I wasn't exactly sure if I should be proud or afraid the boy was defying the laws of human nature.

"Headley, you're amazing."

Not a second after I'd praised Headley, Fred threw up his hands and started wiggling his fingers.

I instantly became worried.

"What's wrong with Fred?"

"Oh, daddy, Fred said that he's amazing, too."

I raised an eyebrow. "How do you know that?"

"I taught him sign language."

The kid's good, I thought. I emitted a drawn-out sigh and gave my attention to my oldest boy.

"Oh, Fred. Yes. You're amazing, too. You'd learned sign language so fast. I am so proud of you and your brother." I kissed both of his hands and moved up to kiss his younger brother on the cheek. "I love you boys, very much."

"Aw...we love you, too, daddy," sighed Headley.

Fred gave me two thumbs up.

The next morning, Mildead's two sisters Sodead and Toodead, were sitting at the kitchen table, whispering to each other. I entered the kitchen from the back door after emptying the trash.

"What are you two whispering about?" I said, being a bit nosy.

Both sisters gazed at me, showing ravenous eyes. "Oh, nothing," answered Sodead.

"Okay, have a good day." I didn't want to spend any more time with them, so I left the kitchen in a flash. I knew they wanted my body, but they weren't going to get it. Only Mildead was allowed anywhere near my sexiness.

"Wait! Filmon, wait up!", yelled Toodead.

Nearing the stairway, I raised my voice, "Um...I gotta go, girls! I gotta go to work!"

But today is Saturday," said Toodead.

I looked back and saw Toodead chasing after me. "Um...I work every day." I was halfway up the stairs when she dove and tackled me.

"Hey! What the... I'm already taken!" I struggled to roll over on my back.

"I'm hungry for you, Filmon," snarled Toodead who was riding me like I was a horse in a rodeo.

"Dammit! It runs in the family!" I shouted.

"Ooh, save me a piece of Filmon, sis!" Sodead exclaimed, standing at the bottom of the stairs.

Toodead bent over and snapped her teeth, nicking me on my ear.

"Aieeeee! You bit me! What's with all the biting in your family!"

I was trying desperately to keep Toodead off of me. I held on to her arms and swayed my head from side to side, avoiding her snapping jaw. She wanted me like a mad sex fiend, and I hadn't even enticed her by doing my sexy dance—head jerk, Running man. Sodead raced up the stairs and held on to my legs and proceeded to take off my shoes and socks. The girl must be into feet, I thought.

"Hey, lee Hilmon alone!" Mildead shouted while standing at the top of the staircase and holding Fred and Headley.

"Yeah! Leave my daddy alone! Get your own boyfriends!" yelled Headley with a fist held high.

Fred repeated Headley's exclamation by signing with fast fingers.

With frustrated expressions, Toodead got off of me, and Sodead released my feet.

Mildead then pointed a long finger toward the front door.

"Now, geh ow ob our howz!"

"Yeah! Get out of our house and hit the road!" Headley added, pointing a shorter finger.

As I was still on my back, I tilted my head to look at Mildead. "But honey, they're your sisters."

"Dey were my shisders."

Without a single word, Toodead and Sodead complied, leaving our house. When the front door closed behind them, I turned to my little family and sighed, knowing that they would always have my back. It was a wonderful feeling.

Baby Boy Pageant

MILDEAD AND I, ALONG WITH Fred and Headley, were in the living room, watching a baby pageant on cable television. I wasn't into it as much as Mildead and the boys were—they hooted and hollered like soccer hooligans, for their favourite babies and toddlers. When the winner was announced, Mildead and Headley promptly booed while Fred gave two thumbs down. Mildead then turned to me and said, "Pred and Headry are cuder dan dat baby."

I quit picking my nose and squinted at the television set. "You know, you're right. Our boys are cuter than that baby." I was aware that Fred and Headley were not your conventional cute babies.

Headley's ears and two of his front teeth were pointed. He kind of looked like Eddie Munster of the 1960's television series The Munsters. As for Fred...at least his hands and legs were cute. *Beauty is in the eye of the bee holder*, my mother had always said.

"Ret's enter Pred an Headry in a baby pageant," uttered Mildead with excitement in her voice.

Thrilled, Headley raised a soprano voice.

"Yeah, daddy! Fred and I will definitely win!"

Fred flicked up two thumbs.

I shot a curious eye at Mildead.

"Are you serious, honey? A baby pageant?"

"Yesh. Pred an Headry hab a great chance to win."

I actually thought it was a good idea. "Okay, why not. Let's enter them in a pageant, baby!"

My little family broke out in cheer and two thumbs up.

Later that night, I went online to check if there were any local baby pageants coming up soon. It took some digging, but I finally found a pageant that was in two weeks and in another city, 50 miles away. There was just one problem. The rules had stated that only one baby per family could enter. I gave the bad news to Mildead and the boys who didn't take it so well. They pouted themselves to sleep.

The next day at work, I couldn't perform my essential duties like I usually did, because all I could think of was how disappointed my little family was last night. I hated to see them that way. So throughout the day, I tried to come up with a solution to our baby pageant dilemma. A solution did come to mind at the end of my shift.

***

On the day of the baby pageant, my nerves were all knotted up. But Mildead didn't seem nervous at all. She was calm as a breastfeeding baby, sitting on the sofa, with a blank expression.

If her eyes hadn't been open, I would've thought she was dead.

As for Fred and Headley, they were more excited than nervous. Fred was doing knee bends as I held his hand, and Headley was shadow boxing.

It was time to suit up.

"All right, boys. Whatever you do, don't take this beanie off," I said, adjusting our secret weapon.

Headley agreed.

"Okay, daddy."

Fred shrugged his shoulders twice.

"What does that mean, Fred?" I asked in a curious voice.

Headley was quick to answer, beating Fred's signing fingers, "Oh, two shrugs mean yes or okay. And one shrug means no."

"Hey, you boys are easy to raise."

Headley and Fred tossed me a smile and a thumbs-up, respectively.

A couple of days ago, I had my friend Janet knit Headley a long green and gold Jamaican/reggae beanie, so to cover the boy's body from the neck down. Therefore, all one could see was Headley's head and Fred's body. But there was a complication: When Fred was upright, it looked like his head (Headley's head) was tilted far to the side.

Before we were about to leave the house for the pageant, I bent over and spoke softly to Headley.

"Son, if anyone asks why you're tilting your head that way, just say you'd slept on the wrong side of the pillow last night."

"Okay, daddy."

I knelt down on one knee and kissed Headley on his forehead, and then I kissed Fred on the knuckles of his hand.

"All right, boys. Are you ready?"

"Yeah!" cheered Headley, as Fred raised both arms. I slapped high-fives to their little hands.

"Let's go win this, baby!"

The baby pageant was being held at a community theatre in the city of Norwood, Ohio. I had entered the boys in the 1-3 years of age division. Although my boys were only seven months old, they were definitely as big as most three-year-olds. There were several categories: best smile; best eyes; most photogenic; and talent. But the prize all parents coveted was the first place trophy, which was awarded to the overall winner.

Mildead and I thought with Fred's athletic body and Headley's head; our boys could sweep all categories. Off-stage, I gave Fred and Headley a pep talk before the commencement of the pageant.

"All right, boys. Be confident and own the stage. And Headley, keep your beautiful smile throughout the pageant. No one has pearly fangs like you, my boy. And Fred, while your brother is singing his song during the talent part, I want you to move your arms and legs in harmony as he sings."

Both boys gave me two thumbs up.

"Daddy, I'm contemplating doing a rap song instead of singing Truly Scrumptious," said Headley.

"But, son. You love Truly Scrumptious. You and your brother watch Chitty Chitty Bang Bang practically every day... Well, what's the name of the rap song?"

"Yo Momma Got Booty."

"Um...I don't think so. Stick with Truly Scrumptious."

"Okay, daddy. You're the boss."

There were around twenty other toddlers competing against my boys as the first event was the best smile category. Mildead wanted me to take Fred and Headley on stage. She thought it would better our chances if I presented the boys before the female judges. Women liked to see fathers interact with their own children. When I carried Fred and Headley onto the stage, I heard giggles and whispers coming from the audience, sensing they were directed toward us. Those narrow-minded adults acted like they hadn't seen a kid wear a Jamaican/reggae beanie before.

We zigzagged our way through the crowd of parents and their babies, to the front of the stage. I wanted the judges to get a good look at my boys, hoping they would appreciate Headley's pretty but tilted head, Fred's energetic body, and of course the Jamaican/reggae culture. I propped Fred up on his feet, with my hands only inches away just in case he needed support. He couldn't walk, but the boy could sure stand without wavering.

I licked my palm and brushed back Headley's silky, jet-black hair.

"All right, son. Smile as you've never smiled before." I bent forward to check out Headley's smile. Perfect. I peered out at the judges and audience, to watch their reactions—most nodded their approval, and then the giggles and whispers eventually turned to positive chatter. Mildead, who was in the front row, sat up straight and puffed out her chest, proud of her son's beautiful smile.

"Atta boy, Headley. Keep smiling, son. And Fred, that's it. Keep it steady, my boy," I praised, grinning like I was a contestant.

The pageant was going well for my boys as the judges seemed to warm up to Headley's charm and Fred's exuberance, all along not having a clue that the tilted-head toddler with a Jamaican/reggae beanie was, in fact, a conjoined twin. The talent category was next, and it was Fred and Headley's turn.

I was sure we would take this event because no other baby in the competition could put an intelligible sentence together much less sing a song.

I once again set the boys at the front of the stage and let them do their thing.

Headley sang like a Broadway star. He moved his tilted head from side to side or up and down, depending on how one is viewing him, and induced some people in the audience to sing along with him.

"Truly scrumptious. You're truly, truly scrumptious. Scrumptious as a cherry peach parfait."

My tears fell when I gazed upon my youngest son singing his favourite song with passion and without inhibition. Then my gaze floated down to my eldest boy who moved his hands with finesse and grace while his feet danced the Two-Step...albeit within a foot radius. I exhaled a deep sigh, for that very moment, the deepest part of my heart anointed me the happiest and proudest father in the world.

Everyone was stunned by Headley's beautiful singing voice, including the judges. They were mesmerized. So was I. When my son sang his last lyric, the audience roared their approval.

"Wonderful job, boys!" Only Fred and Headley heard my voice through the resounding applause.

Finally, it was time for the judges to announce the winners of each category. All the parents and their children were off stage, waiting anxiously for the announcement. The youngest of the female judges, a tall blond with a fake tan, strolled on stage and stood behind a square oak table that presented an assortment of ribbons, envelopes, and one large trophy.

I bent over and whispered in Headley's ear.

"There it is, boys. The winner's trophy."

Headley's eyes were full of hope. "You think we could actually win, daddy?"

"Of course. You boys have an excellent chance." I couldn't take my eyes off that golden statuette of a baby raising its arms in triumph. I visualized the trophy in my arms, cradling it like it was my own child and then handing it to my beautiful, talented boys. An anxious sigh left my body before the judge made her announcement.

The young female judge, who was wearing a navy blue, V-back sheath dress with a slanted pocket jacket, cleared her throat before she spoke

"The winner for the baby with the best eyes is ... Lance Tildon!"

Lance's mother, who stood beside me, turned to me and smirked before she whisked her child on the stage to receive a blue ribbon and an envelope with a $150.00 Toys-4-Tots gift card in it.

As soon as the judge finished presenting the ribbon and envelope to Mrs Tildon and Lance, she made her next announcement.

"And the winner for the most photogenic baby is...Kyle McKinney!"

Mrs McKinney proudly carried her two-year-old boy onto the stage, and she gracefully accepted their ribbon and envelope from the smiling judge.

Headley pouted, "Daddy, aren't Fred and I photogenic?" It broke my heart to hear those words from my own son. I bent down on one knee and replied.

"Heck, yeah. To your mom and I, you and Fred are the most photogenic boys in the whole wide world."

"Thanks, daddy."

Fred then reached up and touched my cheek.

I kissed my two boys at the exact moment the judge made another announcement.

"Our next winning baby won in both the best smile and talent categories."

She cleared her throat before continuing.

"The winner is...Headley Trout!"

"What! We won two, boys!"

I yelled out. And in an instant, I caught my blunder, "I mean...son."

In a flash, the boys and I were in front of the judge, receiving our ribbons and envelopes. Headley beamed a winning smile and Fred couldn't stop clapping.

It wasn't long before the judge was to make her final announcement. She was about to speak, but she turned to the side and eyeballed the boys and I. At first I wasn't sure why she was staring at us, for I was still in happy land. But then I caught on.

"Fred, you can stop clapping now," I whispered.

Fred didn't want to stop. He couldn't untangle himself from the glory of winning. The sound of his clapping echoed throughout the building, but he finally tired himself out and quit.

Satisfied, the judge brought the microphone up to her mouth and began her announcement.

"Now, it's time to name the overall winner of the 11th annual Herman's Donuts baby pageant, boys division."

She paused, roaming her eyes out into the audience. "And the overall winner is...Headley Trout!"

My eyes and mouth stretched wide open. "Yay! We won, boys! We won!" I shouted, swooping Fred and Headley in my arms.

"I knew it, daddy! I just knew it!" Headley shouted as Fred raised his arms in triumph, just like the trophy.

I picked up my boys and started to hug them. I was so happy and proud.

Lance Tildon's mother snubbed her nose and shot me the evil eye.

I had no problem giving her the two-fingered L sign and mouthing loser in silence.

Mildead hopped on the stage and joined in the celebration.

"I knew my shons were buudeepul!"

"That's right, honey," I bellowed. "They're beautiful, all right!"

Then, as I was still jumping with the boys in my arms, Headley's Jamaican/reggae beanie slipped off his body and onto the floor.

"Oh, no!"

There were instant gasps from the audience, followed by shrieking wails. Some people sprang up from their seats, shocked to see a baby with two bodies. I stared out into the audience and saw their horrified expressions. I promptly noticed Headley's own expression—the look of worry and defeat, and Fred's limbs were limp—it was apparent that he, too, felt the same as his brother. Disappointment and sadness seeped from my heart, for no father wanted to see his children unhappy.

The screams withered down to an uneasy hush, prompting the judges to gather and confer with one another. I knew that we were going to be disqualified, so I grabbed Mildead's hand and gave her the keys to the Pacer.

"Honey, go start the car and park it out front," I muttered, still holding the boys in my arms.

Mildead sent me a confused eye before she agreed with a couple of nods, and then she trotted off, stage left.

The host judge clicked on her microphone and spoke with a clear tone.

"Mr Trout...the rules of this baby pageant are quite clear. Only one baby per family is allowed to enter. And conjoined twins are considered two babies. I am sorry. Your twins are disqualified. And all prizes must be returned."

"Daddy, even our ribbons?" asked Headley, pouting a long face.

"Not if I could help it. Hold on, boys." I couldn't bear to see my sons heartbroken, so I did what any father would have done.

Almost any father. I shouted out in the audience and pointed over their heads.

"Look! It's the king of England!"

While I held the boys in one arm, I reached out and snatched the winner's trophy from the judge's table. I then hopped off the stage and made a mad dash for the exit.

"Go, daddy, go!" yelled Headley.

"We're outta here, baby!"

Less than a minute later, with the first-place trophy in the back seat of the car, my little family and I were on our way home, singing one of our favourite songs, "...Oh, you pretty Chitty Bang Bang Chitty Chitty Bang Bang, we love you. And, in Chitty Chitty Bang Bang what we'll do. Near, far, in our..."

CHAPTER 5

Fred and Headley Can Walk

I WAS ALWAYS AMAZED when I would return home from work and find something new going on with my two boys. It was a couple of weeks after the pageant, and as I just entered the front door of my house, Fred came trotting toward me and jumped in my arms.

"Fred, you can walk!" I cried out in awe, and then I began to kiss his palm.

"I can walk, too, daddy," declared Headley.

"What! You can?"

"Yep. You wanna see?"

"Of course."

I set the boys down on the foyer floor.

Fred stepped toward the hallway wall then walked alongside it, leading to the living room. Then Headley stretched out his little legs and started to walk on the wall.

"My boys can walk, baby! Let's celebrate by eating anything you want for dinner and going out for ice cream."

"Yay!" Fred and Headley raced into my arms again.

"What do you boys want to eat?'

Fred signed his choice of food.

"Yeah, steak," added Headley who ate for two, since Fred doesn't have a mouth.

"When did you two start eating steak?"

"This morning. Mommy gave us some of her steaks."

Headley's reply caught me off guard. My boys weren't a year old yet, and they already ate steak.

Also, I have never seen Mildead eat.

"How does mommy eat steak if she doesn't have any teeth?"

"She has false teeth. She puts them on when she eats steak," Headley explained willingly.

"Your mother never told me that."

"Oops. I wasn't supposed to tell," confessed Headley, then he covered his mouth with his hand.

"Why weren't you supposed to tell?"

"Mommy said you liked it when she doesn't have any teeth."

"I only like it in the bedroom when we're doing it. I mean...uh..."

Headley pulled back his head and scrunched up his face.

"Huh?"

"Never mind."

I had to leave the boy hanging. I'll have the "sex talk" with him and his brother when they hit thirty, I said to myself.

After I had spoken to the boys, I asked Mildead if she could prepare a steak dinner for us. She happily obliged. I hadn't mentioned her false teeth because I didn't want to rat on my son for ratting on her. Maybe she had felt bad for biting me during a sexy time when we had just met and didn't want to spur on her kinkiness any longer.

During dinner time, I noticed that Mildead and the boys' steaks were pretty red. I had heard of people who liked their steaks rare, but I had never witnessed anyone eat a rare steak.

It was a pleasant feeling to finally see Mildead eating. "Honey, it's so nice to have you eat a meal with us. You normally say that you're not hungry or you already had eaten. Oh, and I like your new teeth."

Mildead smiled, showing off her dentures.

"When did you get your new teeth?"

"A few months ago," answered Mildead who seemed a bit self-conscious.

It was sure nice to have Mildead speaking English again.

"Oh, all right. They look great, honey."

Mildead smiled at me again as a tiny thread of red meat hung from her front incisors.

"Thank you, Filmon."

Fred and Headley, who were sitting in their highchair, ate their steaks like it was their last meal. Fred grabbed the steak from off the plate and dangled it in the general area where Headley's mouth was at, enticing his little brother to snap at the steak, with his fang-like teeth and swallowing it. Teamwork.

"Honey, you and the boys' steaks look different than mine. Can I taste yours?" I asked, reaching toward her plate, pointing my fork.

"No!" yelled Mildead, pulling her plate away from me.

"Whoa! Excuse me!" I was shocked by her reaction.

"Daddy, you can have some of ours," said Headley.

"No!"

Mildead stretched her body across the table and covered Fred and Headley's plate as her hands knocked over a glass of water.

"Honey, what's wrong with you? It's just a piece of meat."

Mildead, who was still stretched over the table, replied, "It's not the type of meat that you think it is."

"It's not tofu, is it? I hate anything tofu."

Mildead's eyes slanted to the side.

"Uh..."

"What's tofu, daddy?" asked Headley, breaking the tension.

I went on a long and in-depth explanation of the makeup and origins of tofu, eventually forgetting my sharp exchange with Mildead. There were two things that I hated most in the world: Tofu and molten rock. Ugh, I don't even wanna think about them—too many bad memories, I thought. If Mildead and the boys wanted to eat tofu, so be it. *To itch his home*, my mother had always said. If one wished to itch anything, even his or her home, let 'em itch, I was sure that was what she'd meant.

Dinnertime had ended on a positive note, in which Mildead and I had established a more transparent relationship. She and the boys loved tofu meat, and that was fine with me. Also, she had confessed to having new false teeth and was considerate enough not to wear them during sexy time.

The following Saturday, the boys and I spent the afternoon at the park, while Mildead visited her sisters at their new place, near the cemetery. Fred and Headley had been pestering me to buy them a skateboard. It had taken me three days to think about it. They weren't even a year-old yet, and they just learned how to walk. But, since they weren't ordinary boys, I had succumbed to their cuteness and bought them a 22-inch, rainbow-coloured Penny board. Thirty minutes after my boys had received it, they were down the block, cruising toward a nearby park while I followed. I was amazed once again.

It was a lovely afternoon. The brilliant sun spread its warmth upon us as the park's furry and feathered inhabitants scurried about seeking sustenance. A sinuous, concrete path swerved between the Sugar Maple trees, which stood tall, adorning the verdant landscape. Fred and Headley, full of joy,cruised the path with steady progress. It was a sight to see. Fred was on his belly, atop of the skateboard, paddling with his hands while Headley jogged alongside, his little feet tapping the path. I chuckled a bit, for they looked like a rolling boomerang. It was teamwork at its best. I couldn't have been more proud.

I trotted along behind my sons, who were several feet in front of me. They decided to change their positions, in which Fred stood on the skateboard, while Headley dangled in the air, with his arms stretched out, imitating an airplane. On the path, up ahead, were several teenage boys walking toward us. The tallest of the boys held the collar of a massive and menacing-looking Pit Bull Terrier, which began to bark ferociously at my two sons. I wasted no time and swept up Fred and Headley into my arms.

"Daddy, look at the little doggie!" shouted Headley, who apparently seemed unafraid.

The pit bull, only several feet away, was on its hind legs, craving to get at Fred and Headley.

"Could you please keep your dog at a further distance!" I yelled, afraid for my boys.

"Hey, Mister. What in the hell is that?" the teenage dog owner said, seemingly disgusted at the sight of my two sons. The other three boys inched their way toward us to get a closer look at Fred and his brother.

I knew whom the kid was referring to, but I played dumb anyway.

"What?"

The teenage dog owner pointed at my boys.

"That."

"They are my sons, Fred and Headley."

"How do you do?" greeted Headley, smiling.

All four boys seemed startled.

"Whoa! It talks!" the dog owner squawked, as his pit bull drew nearer to us, still barking.

"Hey, get your dog away from us!" I hollered, getting pissed off.

"Hi, wittle doggie. You are so cuuute. Gimme a wittle kissy," said Headley, using a baby voice.

The pit bull became more ferocious and lunged at my sons. I jabbed my hand out to protect my boys, and the dog snapped its jaws, scraping at my palm, missing a full bite. Showing no fear, Headley stretched his head out, inches away from the barking pit bull and forced out a harrowing, cat-like hiss that silenced the monstrous dog in an instant. With its tail between its leg, the pit bull pulled away from its owner and ran off, whining.

"Come back, G.W., come back!" the dog owner cried out. "George Walker!"

All four teenagers scurried away, watching G.W. run further off in the distance.

"Wow, Headley!" I stared into my son's eyes, stunned. "Where did that come from?"

Headley shrugged his shoulders.

"I don't know. I guess it was just instinct. I saw the dog bite you, and I just reacted."

Fred reached up and rubbed his little brother on the head.

I did, too, with an added kiss on the cheek. Later that night, it was Neighbourhood Watch night. Fred and

Headley asked if they could come with me on patrol. I hesitated.

Although I was the chairman of our Neighbourhood Watch program, I was a parent first. So I insisted they wore jackets—children had to dress warmly when the nights were chilly.When it was time to keep the neighbourhood safe, Fred and Headley were on their skateboard, along with nine other adults and me, on the lookout for any criminal activity. We were spread out in the middle of the street, flashlights in hand. Earlier, I had taped a Nite Rider bicycle light to Fred and Headley's skateboard, so to make the boys feel official.

I received a lot of backlash from most of the patrolling adults for bringing Fred and Headley. I thanked them for their concern but reminded them that I was the chairman of this outfit. I did feel a bit of guilt for having to slam the hammer down on subordinates, yet a leader had to do what he had to do.

I was going to tell them about the pit bull incident with Headley, to establish the boy's credentials as a tough crime fighter, but I decided against it, for leaders didn't have to explain anything. We expected all those who were below us in rank to just follow orders and nothing else.

If I wanted my nearly one-year-old twins to patrol the streets at night and in the cold, looking for criminals, then doggone it, they were going to patrol the streets.

The adults soon gave in to my authority, and they allowed the subject to die. But they brought the issue up again when Fred and Headley kept taking potty breaks. Then one of my bold, patrolling subordinates challenged my authority.

"Come on, Filmon. Your boys are just toddlers. What if a bunch of Los Angeles rap hoodlums did a drive-by and busted caps in our asses?" said Harold, who was a junior-high-school science teacher.

I gave Harold a sideways glance.

"Then, we'd be in Los Angeles. But since we're not in Los Angeles, my boys will patrol the streets with the rest of us. My authoritative decree still stands."

"Oh, brother," Harold muttered.

"Daddy, look! Criminals!" Headley yelled, pointing to a couple of dark figures running away from an old man who lived down the block from me.

I blew my crime whistle to alert the others who proceeded to blow their own whistles. "Hey, you two, stop!" I screamed. "I'm the Neighbourhood Watch chairman, and I command you to stop!"

The two shadowy figures kept on running, then one of them raised a hand.

"I think one of the criminals waved goodbye," I said, flustered. "The criminal gave you the Finger, daddy," Headley replied.

"Oh..."

We were about to give chase but instead rushed to aid the old man who sat gingerly on the curb.

He held his left shoulder, in obvious pain. I took out my cell phone and called 911.

"Sir, I just called the police...and an ambulance should be here shortly," I said to the old man, sincerely concerned. "Were you shot or stabbed?"

The old man gave me a sharp reply.

"No. The broad bit me."

Although he seemed to be in his 70's, I noticed that he was in good shape for his age, he had Popeye arms hanging from broad shoulders. The only clothing he had on was white BVDs underwear.

"You mean a woman bit you?"

"That's what I just said. Are you deaf?"

"There's no need to be snippy, sir. I'm just trying to get the facts."

The old man squinted at me.

"Are you a policeman?"

"Not exactly. But the police force and I are somewhat related. My name is Filmon Trout. And I hold an elite position in our Neighbourhood Watch program. I live up the block from you."

The old man rolled his eyes.

"Two women broke into my house as I was sleeping. One of them jumped on my bed and held my legs. And the other one bit me, taking a small chunk outta my shoulder. I...I somehow overpowered them...and then they ran out of my house. I think that one broad was trying to eat me. Damn, cannibal broads."

The old man took his hand away from his shoulder to check on his wound.

I shone the flashlight on the old man's shoulder, near the armpit. Partial teeth marks were carved into his skin, along with a bloody gash, an inch in diameter.

"She got you good, sir. What did they look like?" I asked, with my eyes still on the old man's wound.

"They were funny looking—really pale and a bit green. And they looked like twins."

Both Fred and Headley, who were behind me, pulled on my pant leg.

"Daddy," Headley whispered. Then the boy used a come-hither finger to get me to bend an ear. My eyes kept widening while I listened to my youngest son.

"I think they were aunties Toodead and Sodead."

"Are you sure?" I asked in a whisper.

Headley returned a slight nod.

The old man rubbernecked, and his jaws dropped when Fred and Headley came into his view. He shook off his daze and caught my own bewildered countenance.

"What's the matter? Do you know those women?" the old man asked me.

I wanted to tell him that I was pretty sure the culprits were my girlfriend's sisters, Toodead and Sodead. But for some reason, I couldn't bring myself to rat on them. After all, they were my children's aunts.

"Um...was one of them wearing a nurse's outfit?"

The old man nodded.

"Yes."

"And the other, a rainbow-coloured top?"

"Yes. That's the one who bit me!"

The old man jumped to his feet.

"You know them?"

"Nope...don't know 'em. Sorry, gotta go. I hope you feel better, sir. Let's go, boys." I puckered up my lips and started to whistle as guilt plastered my face. Then I used quick steps toward my house while Fred and Headley rolled alongside me, struggling to keep up.

As soon as we got home, I went straight to the bedroom to have a talk with Mildead about her bite-happy sisters. She wasn't there. I'd forgotten that on certain nights she would go out early in the evening and did her own patrolling of the neighbourhood. Mildead had insisted that she go out alone.

Who was I to be in the way of women's lib? At 4 in the morning, Mildead finally showed up; I awoke to the rustling of bed sheets. I never asked Mildead why she patrolled the streets for hours; I just took it as her being committed to the cause. I thought that was so sexy.

When I rubbed the sleep from my eyes, I spoke to Mildead about her sisters biting the old man.

Mildead spoke in a monotone.

"I'm sorry, Filmon. I'll talk to them tomorrow."

"Okay. And I don't want your sisters in our house or neighbourhood anymore."

"Yes. Filmon."

I wish she'd tell me where she went at night, I mumbled to myself. At least her enunciation had improved and certainly appreciated.

CHAPTER 6

Fred and Headley's First Birthday and First Day At School

WEEKS AGO MILDEAD AND I had planned to give the boys a grand party, fitting for one-year-olds. But that soon changed when Fred and Headley had grown at a rapid pace. At a year old, not only were Fred and Headley as big as five-year-olds, they were baby geniuses. Fred was a sign language wiz and already a nimble-bodied wonder. He could do backflips and front flips like an Olympic gymnast, though his baby brother could do without the flips—made him nauseous. As for Headley, the boy was a student of many subjects, especially linguistics. Recently, he had learned to speak fluent Swahili in just two days.

"Why Swahili, son?" I said curiously.

"I wanted to learn the language of parts of Africa, my Motherland," he replied.

"But you're not black."

"We all black, daddy."

Headley's we all black remark intrigued me enough to visit the genealogy library the next day. I always respected my son's genius.

And it was true. A relative of years ago, the gay Chinese railroad worker who was half Apache, had a second cousin named Ming Lee, who also happened to be his aunt, and who had sexual relations with a black slave who'd often contended he had a gay nephew somewhere living in Apache territory. Put two and nine together—thus, the African blood in our family.

Fred and Headley's birthday finally arrived. I invited all my neighbours, but none of them showed up. Bastards. I'd given everyone the heads up over a month ago, sending out invitations with large,black-embossed letters, You Are Invited To Fred And Headley's First Birthday On Sunday, December 25th at 10 am. Be There Or Be Square, so to give them more than enough time to fit my boys' birthday into their schedules. When I see those neighbours of mine, they better have a good excuse why they hadn't shown up, I said to myself, ticked off.

I was happy and appreciative when my friend Janet arrived at 10 am sharp. A good friend, indeed. She brought a guy with her, the man dressed as a clown, but we later had to ask the poor fellow to take his costume and makeup off because he scared the bazeebas out of Headley. That shocked me.

The boy had no fear of ferocious pit bulls, but for some reason, he was terrified of clowns. Since Janet and the clown guy were our only guests, we were stuck with an abundance of food that was enough for at least 50 people.

I soon excused myself, leaving Janet and clown guy to listen to Headley's knock-knock jokes. I returned thirty minutes later with seven homeless guys. It was a tight fit in the Pacer, but the homeless were used to that sort of thing. At 1 pm, the Mariachi band I had hired finally showed up. Fred and Headley loved Mariachi music. The band was supposed to show up at 10:45 am to set up and perform at 11:30. But two of the members who were non-binary lesbians eloped to Mexico early in the morning. That left only two Mariachi band members.

Fred and Headley didn't show any disappointment that a full band hadn't shown up. They would have been happy if only one band member had arrived. Yet I wasn't pleased. I just wanted my boys to experience what a birthday party should be like—full band, a bunch of guests, non-threatening clowns, etc. However, soon fortune was among us. Two of the homeless men were brothers; once famous Mexican singing stars Paco y Taco. When the two brothers, gracious in bearing, heard about the short-handed Mariachi band, they offered their services to sing.

Hard times had befallen the two brothers when their manager had embezzled all their money. Paco and Taco had been devastated. Soon drugs and alcohol had consumed them. Then one day, in a drunken stupor, they'd made a run for the border, in the hope of becoming the first undocumented Mexican brothers to represent the Republican party and run for senators in the state of Texas. Within a week of crossing the border, their aspirations were squashed, when a small band of Republicans had mistaken the two brothers for being left-wing Iraqis and ran them out of the state. The two brothers had then hitched a ride, ending up homeless in Ohio.

When it was time for the band to play, Paco and Taco sang like the famous duo they once were, harmonising with melodious notes and full of passion. They had one and all dancing together in my backyard patio, except for Janet who respectfully kept her distance since the pungent odour of grime and urine was too much for her. An hour later, the band finished their set in front of appreciative applause and cheers that lasted a good minute. Paco y Taco was back. Ariba!

Fred and Headley finally opened their birthday gifts. Janet's gifts to the boys were two paint by number kits and two Nintendo Game Boys. The homeless guys, bless their hearts, pooled their resources together and sent one of their own to the corner liquor store to buy Fred and Headley a birthday gift. The poor guy must have lost his way because he hadn't returned. Mildead and I bought the boys a specially-made tricycle, in which Fred peddled, while Headley steered tilted, oversized handlebars.

The boys loved their gifts and seemed to enjoy themselves. Overall, it was a great first birthday.

Since Fred and Headley were developing much faster than normal children, Mildead and I decided to send them to school. Headley loved the idea and couldn't wait. But Fred didn't take it so well.

He signed his displeasure with speedy fingers, and then he gave me the Finger.

"Fred, who taught you the Finger?" I snapped.

Fred pointed a long, index finger upward to rat on his brother.

I sent Headley a sidelong glance. "Headley, shame on you. I didn't teach you the Finger so that you could teach it to Fred. Now cover your ears. I need to talk to your brother alone."

I kissed Fred's hand before I spoke to him, "Why don't you want to go to school, son?"

Fred shrugged his shoulders and lifted his hands, palms up.

"He thinks all the kids will make fun of him, daddy," Headley intervened.

"Didn't I tell you to cover your ears."

"Sorry, daddy." Headley plugged his ears, using his two pinkie fingers like I had used to do.

I returned my attention to Fred and gazed at the San Francisco 49er insignia on the front of his little football jersey. "I'm not going to lie you, son. I will never lie to you. There will be some kids who won't understand your beauty and will indeed make fun of you because they've been raised to be butthole jerks like their parents. But there'll definitely be kids who'll be your friends." I held both of Fred's hands. "And school is cool, son. Come on. You wanna go?"

Fred lifted his shoulder once for a no.

"Come on, son. You'll like school."

An even harder shoulder lift from Fred.

"Fred, you know you're connected to your brother, right?"

Two shoulder lifts for a yes.

"Therefore, if your brother goes to school, you're going, too. It's the law, and that's final."

There was an emphatic shoulder lift and the Finger.

"Whatever, Fred."

Fred finally came around and agreed to go to school. It took some expert parenting and child psychology manoeuvring to get him to agree. But what won him over was that I had promised he would someday be first in line to inherit my orange 1978 Pacer. When one was that young and inexperienced, any car was cool.

The first day of school was an eventful day for everyone. Although it was the only kindergarten in the public school system, I dressed the boys in private-school uniforms so that they could stand out more among the other children. Fred and Headley looked so cute in their little matching outfits. Each boy wore a teal vest coat over a white shirt, and their tiny black shorts were several inches above the knee, while long, white socks ran down their legs, meeting black loafers.

Headley frowned.

"What's the matter, son?"

"Daddy, we look like little German boys wearing lederhosen, ready to climb the Swiss Alps."

"Get outta town. You boys look smart. And how do you know what German boys wear? These lee...der...ho—"

Headley rolled his eyes. "Lederhosen. German for leather breeches."

I was confused once again.

"Shorts, daddy."

"Oh... Hey, what's all this German stuff, anyway?"

"Yesterday, I started to learn the German language. I should be fluent in a couple of days."

Maybe I should have the boys skip kindergarten, my mind said.

Mildead thought it would be best if I took the boys to school. She had a problem with her sense of direction. Plus, she was a terrible driver. The last time Mildead had driven the Pacer, I was asleep in the passenger seat. She was supposed to have dropped me off at work, but we'd somehow ended up crossing the Canadian border. Before that, while still in the driveway, she had driven the car around in circles and had come back in the house twenty minutes later, complaining that she couldn't find the supermarket. Fortunately, Fred and Headley had saved us time and gas in the future by ratting her out.

Mildead's driving privileges have since been terminated.

Mildead kissed the boys and me goodbye. Since we'd met, she'd never been too emotional. Though after she kissed the boys, her eyes welled up. It was a moment that touched my heart, and since I've always been an emotional sort, I cried like a baby. I didn't want them to go anymore. I started to take the boys' uniforms off, so to put their pyjamas back on, until Headley bopped me on the head, barking at me to man up. I eventually played off my sissiness and told the boys that I was kidding around, and neither kid bought it.

Mercy primary school was located in downtown Beavercreek. Therefore it was a short drive, three-quarters of a mile away from my home. Mercy consisted of five bungalows. Three of the bungalows, B, C, and D, each held a maximum of twenty children. Bungalow A was the administrative office, and Bungalow E was for the intolerable kids, I had spent most of my primary school years there. Two separate playgrounds fronted the bungalows, which were aligned together in U-shaped fashion, along with fenced-off miniature gardens, located at the rear of each building.

I held Fred's hand, leading the boys to their kindergarten class, bungalow B. Class had already started, and we were late because the boys wouldn't get into the car. They had been arguing about who was going to sit shotgun. Fred had always sat tall in the front seat, while Headley rested his feet on the upper back support. Yet Headley had argued and ranted that since he was of mature age and body, he should finally have the opportunity to sit in the front seat. Fred had responded with animated gestures, mostly giving his brother the Finger. Stopping those two boys from arguing was like trying to lasso a tornado.

Frustrated, I had to put my foot down to stop the madness. However, I had done it literally and too hard, slightly spraining my ankle. We had lost a lot of time looking for an Ace bandage, to wrap up my foot. Finally, Fred had given in and allowed his brother to sit in the front seat. It had been a feat to behold. Fred had slumped over upside down, atop the seat's back support, allowing Headley to sit upright, which he had never done before. More teamwork.

The door to bungalow B was held open by a doorstop. Around eighteen children sat in class, with their backs to the door, listening to a young female teacher who held up a large picture of a horse, over her head.

On the blackboard, behind the teacher, was her name written in chalk: Miss Colt. She smiled when her eyes met mine, and when her sights dropped down a couple of feet, laying upon Fred and Headley, the smile she just had evolved to a gape of the mouth.

The children witnessed their teacher's transformation, and they followed her eyes to whatever was behind them.

"Hello, there. I'm Mr Trout. And let me introduce my two sons, Fred and Headley. They—"

Two little girls screamed, and one boy ran behind the teacher. Within seconds every kid started to cry. I was stunned by their reactions. At first, I thought they were afraid because there was a strange man in their class. Then a little boy pointed at Fred and Headley and shouted.

"Monster kids!"

I was astounded and hurt from the little brat's words. "No, they aren't monsters. My sons are just like you all but smarter. They are Siamese twins, connected. And..."

The kids weren't listening to me, and they were still crying and screaming.

"Calm down, children," Miss Colt sounded off, "calm down. There's nothing to be afraid of, Fred and Har..." Miss Colt looked to me, unsure of Headley's name.

"Headley!" I raised my voice, correcting her.

She continued, "... Fred and Headley are two kids...." Miss Colt glanced at me once again. "They are two boys, right?"

"Yes, they are two separate beings," I replied, getting annoyed.

She returned her attention to the frightened children. "They are two kids who look a little different. So please, stop crying and welcome Fred and Headley to our class."

Every single child shook their head, then their cries and whimpers turned to sudden wails.

Miss Colt raised her voice louder through the din. "Mr Trout. I am truly sorry. But you must take your boys away. The children are just too afraid right now. Maybe you could come another time."

Headley pouted and asked, "Daddy, we can't go to school?"

I set my eyes down on Headley's pitiful face and replied. "Not today, son. We'll come back, maybe tomorrow." I turned around and began to walk the boys out of the class. I then bent down and spanked Fred on the butt, for giving the kids and Miss Colt a parting middle finger.

On the way back home, with Fred happily riding shotgun again, I asked the boys how they were doing. Fred was elated that he didn't have to go to school, but Headley was obviously hurt. He had looked forward to going to school and be around other kids.

"Headley, maybe it's a good thing that you and your brother don't attend kindergarten. You two are much too smart to be in any primary school." I stated a truth, and I wanted to relieve Headley of the doldrums.

"I guess you're right, daddy. But why were those kids so scared like that? I thought they'd make fun of us, instead of being afraid of us."

At that moment, I wanted to hold my two boys in my arms, but I was driving. "Son, they acted like that because you and your brother are dif...unique. They just never seen anyone like you and your brother before. Hey, I'd never seen anyone like you and your brother before."

Fred jumped in and signed with his speedy fingers again, asking if I had been afraid when they were born.

"No, son. I wasn't afraid. I was just surprised, that's all. But not even a little afraid. I thought you two were beautiful and special. And I will always feel that way. I love you both so much."

"We love you, too, daddy," said Headley, extending a soft grin.

Fred promptly followed with two thumbs up.

I soon realised that sending Fred and Headley to school wouldn't be in their best interests. I didn't want my boys to be the objects of ridicule or feel depressed because of the frightened or ignorant reactions from others. I decided my boys would be better off homeschooled. Headley had already been schooling himself and Fred, reading any literature he could find. I would have to buy them more textbooks or audios on anything educational.

Furthermore, if they would like to follow in my footsteps as Wildlife Waste Handlers, which I expect them to do, I would educate them on the art of detecting all types of animal faeces, their smell, texture and colour. That would be a great day if my sons decided to work alongside me, scooping up faeces from off the ground, examining and smelling it for animal research purposes. Nevertheless, no matter what employment they'd procure, I'd still be the proudest father on earth.

CHAPTER 7

Fugitives From Justice

Since it was an icy-cold evening in the Beavercreek area, my little family and I decided to stay in from patrolling the neighbourhood and watch a movie on TV. While the boys and I were waiting for the Movie of the Week, "Zombie Love" a romantic horror flick, Mildead brought me a large tub of popcorn, and the boys, a snack of that nasty faux ... tofu meat in little chunks, with toothpicks pricked in them.

I did have my reservations about Fred and Headley eating that meat, but they seemed to enjoy it, and they haven't had any side effects yet. Also, they weren't dead or anything, so what kind of father would I be if I deprived them of life's little pleasures.

"Daddy, why do you always keep the same popcorn tub, after we see a movie in the theatre?" Headley asked.

I waited until I swallowed a mouthful of popcorn before answering.

"For the free refills. So the next time we go to the theatre, I'll take this tub and get a free refill of popcorn, baby."

Headley scrunched up his face, the same way his mother did whenever they were confused about something like they had bowel problems. "But...daddy, isn't multiple refills, stealing?"

I was always appreciative and proud whenever my sons had caught me doing something wrong. But since I'm the head of the household, head honcho, numero uno around here, I exerted my autonomous power on my little boy, and I came up with a trivial excuse for being shamed with the truth.

"Hey, there's no sign anywhere in the theatre that states one couldn't keep the same popcorn tub for future refills. But there is a sign that states—free refills with every purchase of a large popcorn tub. That's refills with an S."

"I don't think there's an S after refill on any of the theatre menus, daddy. I'm pretty sure of it."

"Hmm...you may be right... Yep, it's stealing. But you two boys never do what I do when it comes to popcorn tub refills, hear me."

"Okay, daddy."

I turned the channel on the television, catching the last part of the news before Zombie Love came on at 7 pm. Mildead sat down with the boys on the sofa, while I kicked back in my usual spot on the leather recliner. Channel 7 News showed the tail end of a feel-good story, in which an Australian transexual dwarf who'd recently moved to Ohio, had reunited with his/her dingo after five years. As soon as that segment was over, the words Breaking News flashed on the TV screen. Two seconds later, video pics of Mildead's sisters appeared before us.

"Daddy, it's aunties Toodead and Sodead!" Headley announced.

My interest peaked after the initial shock. "Oh, my... Okay, shh...be quiet. Let's hear what's goin' on."

Carolyn Yates, channel seven news anchor, reported the shocking news of Mildead's sisters:

Two women in their mid to late 20's are at large tonight. They are suspected of biting at least seven people, in a rash of assaults that were committed in the past forty-eight hours. One victim had his finger bitten off after he tried to defend himself. If anyone has any information to the whereabouts of these women, contact the police department immediately. In other local news:

after forty years since its grand opening, the Crest, the only movie theatre in Beavercreek, had to close its doors today due to bankruptcy. The heartbroken owners had attributed the down-ward-spiralling popcorn sales as the blame for their demise."

Stunned from the news of the Crest's closing, I turned to Mildead and addressed the minor issue, regarding Toodead and Sodead. "Honey, what's up with all this biting crap with you and your sisters?"

Without saying anything, Mildead just shrugged her shoulders.

"Were you and your sisters always biting people ever since you were children?"

Mildead shook her head.

"When did it all start?" I sensed my questioning was bothering her.

Mildead hopped up from the sofa and cried out, "I can't tell you, Filmon! I just can't!" Then she marched with quick steps toward the front door.

"Hey, where you going?" I called out.

"Out patrolling."

My first thought was that she was dedicated to the cause, but I soon realised how emotional she had been. The first time she had been that emotional was when she had just given birth to Fred, and when the doctors had wanted to take the baby away to examine him. The inner workings of my acute intellect were bustling with activity. There was something clearly going on with Mildead. I couldn't put the finger on it just yet though my mastery of deduction was beginning to set its course.

My mind immediately went to work: Mildead and her sisters may indeed be foreign agents of sorts, biting as many American citizens as they could—to weaken the nation's infrastructure. And Mildead, whose motherly instincts kicked in, had ceased her mission because she'd given birth to the boys. Genius! Like sons like father.

The next morning at breakfast, I asked Mildead, as the boys listened on if she was, in fact, a foreign spy.

Mildead busted out in laughter. "That's so ridiculous, Filmon!"

The boys then joined in the hilarity. "You're funny, Daddy," said Headley, as Fred held his tummy, laughing within.

My mind floundered, and thought, okay, cross the spy thing out.

Throughout the day, I came up with subtle ways to get Mildead to open up about her past. She knew what I was trying to do and kept mum, dodging my indirect questions at every turn. At the end of the day, I knew where Fred had gotten his stubbornness. I gave up. If she wanted to tell me in her own time what was going on with her personal life, so be it. I'm sure she would come around and tell me someday.

The next afternoon, which was a Sunday, the police were going door to door, asking questions about Sodead and Toodead. They were investigating the biting assault of the old man who lived down the street. In addition, someone had told the police that two women who had matched Sodead and Toodead's description, had exited my house a few months ago. A detective Samuels, with worn-out eyes and a thick neck, began to question Mildead and I. Since I wasn't comfortable ratting on Mildead's sisters, I denied knowing them.

"Mr Trout, are you sure you haven't seen these two women before? Take a look at the pictures again," said detective Samuels, who kept a keen eye on Mildead at the same time.

It troubled me that I had to lie to the police. If Sodead and Toodead were foreign spies, I would have given them up in a second, but I needed to hear from Mildead first if the biting sickness in their family was related to her strange behaviour. "Yep, detective, I'm sure…. I haven't seen these women before."

Detective Samuels narrowed his eyes at Mildead and said, "Ma'am, you have a striking resemblance to the two women in question."

Mildead began to fidget.

"I…I—" I butted in for the save.

"Um...I think they wear the same makeup, detective. Green foundation makeup is popular with women these days."

The detective seemed to grasp my explanation in hand, then thanked us for our cooperation. Before he stepped out of the front door, detective Samuels wheeled around and gave Mildead one last, hard glance. I didn't like the way the detective had eyeballed Mildead. He seemed suspicious; I had to throw him off again.

"Honey, you must change your makeup to the colour it was before. I liked it when it was black."

I shut the door behind the detective, unsure my remark would stop him from sniffing around again.

I peered through the front door window and watched detective Samuels drive away. Then I swung around and shot Mildead a stern eye.

"Honey, I lied to the police. I hate lying. Now you must tell me what's going on with you and your sisters biting people. Are you in some kinda cult or something?"

Mildead seemed nervous. I sensed a deep secret within her.

"Filmon, I don't know how—"

Suddenly, the front door flew open, hitting the foyer wall with a hard thud, then Fred and Headley darted into the house.

"Hi, mommy. Hi, daddy," said Headley. "You two look pretty serious."

"Boys, didn't I tell you not to open the door like that. I want you two to leave your mother and me alone to talk. Go upstairs and clean up your room." I sounded off, feeling a bit irritated.

"That's okay, Filmon. They know." Mildead said softly.

"Huh? Know what?"

"What I am."

I folded my arms and bent my head forward. "What do you mean, what you are?"

"Mommy's a zombie, daddy," Headley declared.

I burst out laughing. Headley must've gotten his sense of humour from my brother Zeke, who was always joking around. "A zombie...funny, son."

Mildead reached out and rubbed my shoulder. "It's true, Filmon. I am a zombie. My sisters and I had turned into the living dead two years ago. We—"

"Hold up. I'm being Punk'd right now, or I'm on Candid Camera, right?" I started to look around the house for hidden cameras.

"Daddy, mommy's telling the truth. She is a zombie. And Fred and I are half zombies."

Mildead held both of my hands and spoke softly, "I wanted to tell you when Fred and Headley were born, but I was afraid you would leave me."

"Wait." I held up an open hand. "You're serious? You're a zombie?"

Mildead drew me in closer, touching my cheek, using her cold fingers. "Yes, Filmon. I am a zombie."

I'd thought she was going to say that she was French. I stayed quiet for a good ten seconds in absolute shock and disbelief. Part of me wanted to run away, but my family was everything to me. I had little love in my life until Mildead and the boys had come along.

"I need to sit down." I moved to the living room and sat on the sofa since it was closer to me than my recliner. Mildead sat next to me, as the boys knelt at my feet and seemed to wonder what I was going to say or do. I gazed into Mildead's semi-bloodshot eyes and questioned her.

"So, you eat people?" I said, still in a state of disbelief.

Mildead held my hands again.

"Yes. And animals, too."

"Hold your whores! You mean to tell me that you ate my two hamsters, Timmy and Jimmy? And my cat Charlie?"

"I'm sorry, Filmon. But it was either them or you. At the time, I was beginning to like you, so I just ate the animals."

I held my heart, and I thought I had a heart attack. "Oh, no. Poor Timmy, Jimmy, and Charlie. I thought some weirdo had kidnapped them. And then I'd hoped they had run away together to a park or a zoo, trying to put the kidnapping outta my head."

Mildead tried her best to console me by rubbing both of my shoulders. "I'm sorry. I'm so sorry, Filmon."

"What about our neighbour Mary's missing son? Did you eat him, too?"

"Yes. But—"

"Oh, my god, it's true! My babies' momma is an eater of men!"

Mildead hit herself on the hip. "Filmon, he tried to force himself upon me!"

I snapped out of my overly dramatic stupor.

"What?"

"He had grabbed me from behind and then knocked me to the ground. And...then he jumped on top of me..."

I sat up erect. "Did Mary's son had his way with you?"

"No. I bit his neck and tore open his throat. He was dead in less than two seconds," Mildead nonchalantly replied.

"Phew...good," I said with relief.

"You're not mad, Filmon?"

"No. He was a bad man. He went to prison for assaulting women. I'm surprised they'd let him out."

"Yep, he got what he deserved. Gimme a high 5."

Mildead obliged me with a soft high 5. I picked up Fred and Headley, placing them on my lap. Then I put my arm around Mildead's shoulders and showed her a sincere facial expression.

"Okay, tell me everything."

Mildead nodded in agreement. "About two years ago, not too long before we met, my sisters and I were driving along the freeway and picked up a hitchhiker. So—"

"So...he was the zombie," I chimed, interrupting.

"No. The hitchhiker was just some cute guy we'd picked up."

"Then what does he have to do with the story?"

"Daddy, mommy's getting there," said Headley, who never took his eyes off his mother.

I bent over and looked at Headley's profile.

"Hey, have you heard this story before?"

"Yes, daddy...a few times."

I turned to Mildead. "You told the boys and not me?"

"I wasn't sure you'd understand."

"You got that right, sister... Okay, go on with your story."

Mildead took in a deep breath and continued, "Well, after we made out with the hitchhiker. We—"

"What! You all had sexual relations with him?"

"No. No. We just took turns kissing."

I held up a wide palm. "This is pre-zombie, right?

"Yes, of course." Mildead gave me that scrunched up look of hers again.

"...Cause, you girls have a frisky, post-zombie reputation, you know."

Mildead rolled her eyes at me. "Anyway..."

"Anyway," I repeated, mocking her.

"Cool it, you two! Can we get on with the story, please?" groaned Headley.

I twisted my mouth. "You already heard it."

"I know. But I like to hear stories, daddy."

I leaned back on the sofa and yielded.

"Okay. Okay. Honey, go on."

"Anyway..." Mildead glanced at me sideways.

I gave her a partial evil eye.

Mildead went on.

"After we'd dropped off the hitchhiker, we'd pulled in at a rest stop. And there, we'd met a young couple, Jerry and Anne—"

"So they were zombies."

"No."

"Oh, brother." I was starting to regret my inquisition.

"Jerry and Anne had introduced us to a man who they had just met, and who'd desperately needed a ride—"

"All right, he was the zombie."

Mildead gave me a firm nod. "Yes."

"Finally... Now, why didn't Jerry and Anne give that zombie fellow a ride?"

"They were on a motorcycle."

"Oh. All right, you give this guy a ride, and he bites you and your sisters in the car, turning all three of you into zombies."

"No."

"Oy vey! I'm getting a migraine," I complained, holding my temples.

"We made out with him first, and then he invited—"

"What...the.... You kissed a zombie!"

Mildead folded her arms. "So did you. And, you had sex with one."

"Oh, yeah. Never mind."

"Anyway..." There was that exasperated look again. "He invited us to his place at the cemetery,and it was there...he had bitten us, turning us into zombies."

"I love that story, mommy," sighed Headley.

Fred clapped several times and gave his mother two thumbs up.

"Wait up, I hadn't seen any bite marks on you," I said.

Mildead bent down and showed me the back of her head.

She then kneaded her hair apart, revealing a four-inch diameter hole.

I screamed like a little girl.

"Aieeee! Oh, my goodness! Are you okay?"

"Of course, Filmon. I don't feel any pain. I'm dead."

I started to scratch my head, still overwhelmed by what I had just heard. Then a puzzling thought popped up inside my mind.

"Hey, why aren't I a zombie, too? You had bitten me on the arm, and your sister Toodead and knicked me on the ear."

"Our bites hadn't penetrated through your skin, drawing blood." Mildead sounded like a medical examiner.

"Oh, Okay. I'm just having trouble believing you guys are...I mean...I don't know what I mean. All this, it just seems unreal." I grew quiet again. My brain wanted me to flee, but my heart wanted me to remain and work it out. And since I rarely listen to my mind, which is overrated, I decided to stick with my zombie family. "All right, I've made a decision."

Mildead and the two boys leaned in closer to me, with anxious looks on their faces.

"Mildead, I love you and the boys very much. I've never been happier since you three came into my life. Zombie or not, I will support you, honey."

Mildead threw her arms around me. "Oh, Filmon, that means so much to me." Fred and Headley joined in, making it a group hug. "We love you, daddy."

For a long moment, I basked in the love from my little family, holding them tight. It felt beautiful, yet I did have reservations about Mildead eating people.

"All right. Honey, I know you have to eat. But does it have to be human flesh?"

"Yes. Although I prefer human brains, and I could only eat animal flesh for so long. But then my cravings for human flesh would be unbearable. After two weeks of having no human flesh or brains, I wouldn't be able to control myself, and I'd probably eat any human that was near me, including you, Filmon."

I gulped hard.

"And that goes for Fred and Headley, too," Mildead resumed.

My eyebrows hit the top of my head. "What do you mean, Fred and Headley, too?"

"The boys also need to eat human flesh and brains."

"Now hold your whores! But they're not the living dead!"

"Ha! ha! You repeated it. It's hold your horses. Not whores," Headley corrected me, "you're funny, daddy."

Fred held his tummy while his shoulders shook—the boy was laughing his little butt off.

Mildead continued. "True. They are not the living dead. But they desperately crave human flesh and brains just as I do. I've been feeding them human flesh twice a week."

"You mean that faux tofu meat is human flesh?" Mildead tilted her head and nodded reluctantly.

I tightened my lips and let out a hard breath through my nose. "All right. From now on, no more lies or secrets among us. Also, I understand that you three must have human flesh. So..."

"And brains, daddy," Headley added.

I winced, and then I concurred, "And brains..."

Fred patted the top of Headley's head and flicked up a thumb.

I proceeded on, facing Mildead. "Honey, you had the right idea to whack and eat our neighbour's son, he was definitely a bad seed. Therefore, we will only execute and eat bad people. Is that clear to everybody?"

Headley looked at me with hopeful eyes. "You're gonna eat bad people too, daddy?"

"No way. Just you three. You're the zombies...just do what you all do, and if you guys need any help, let me know. Now, remember, only whack bad people, okay?"

Mildead and Headley nodded going while Fred clapped.

Man, I can't believe I'm now the head of a vigilante zombie family, I never saw that coming.

A week passed since Mildead had confessed that she was a zombie; I thought I'd undoubtedly have nightmares of her eating me as I slept. On the contrary, I've been sleeping much better lately, and our sexy time has perked up a bit, too. But I wasn't sure how I'd feel about being complicit as my zombie family ate an unwitting lousy person, to appease their uncontrollable cravings. I had never committed a crime in my life until I lied to the police about not knowing Sodead and Toodead. Even though I'd told Mildead only to eat bad people, the thought still bothered me. I needed to combat my reservations with a vigilante mindset and a sense of urgency.

Wicked people had to be eaten so my little family could survive. There were many benefits to eating bad people: it saved money on groceries; it cuts crime, and we taxpayers would save heaps of cash by not incarcerating them. In some states, it costs taxpayers nearly $50,000 per year to incarcerate an inmate. That was twice my salary as a Wildlife Waste Handler. Alas, to be so undervalued and unappreciated by the world, I said to myself, sighing.

As I again began to psyche myself up, a sense of empowerment flowed throughout my being. I had three executioners of villains under my power. All in the name of morality. Our new crusade was about to be sent forth to battle evil. I believed that I was at the helm to lead my zombie family on a dangerous quest to rid the world of wickedness, tyranny, and improper behaviour.

Bad People Taste Better

I DISCUSSED THE NOTION of battling evil in other parts of the country, and possibly the world to Mildead and the boys. They loved it. Especially, the boys who deemed my vision as an adventure. Mildead was more practical about it—she was just glad that I supported her eating people. But before we headed out into the world in search of wickedness, I wanted to invite Janet to our farewell dinner since she was my best friend and the boys' godmother. Although I would have to keep her in the dark about the reason for our family's departure, not a soul would have an inkling of our mission, which would be a thankless and most challenging undertaking. We were soon to be covert heroes for humankind.

Before Janet arrived for our farewell dinner, Headley wanted to have a word with me regarding his future meals.

"Daddy, I decided only to eat bad French people."

He caught me off guard with that remark. "Um, why only French people, son?"

Headley just shrugged his shoulders.

I thought about pushing the boy to elaborate because I felt there was a reason for him wanting to eat only bad French people, but who was I to understand the mind of a boy genius. I turned my attention to his older brother, who had his arms folded. "Fred, how do you feel about that?"

Fred showed me a thumbs down and the Finger, using both hands.

"Fred, a thumbs down will do. There's no need to ac-cent your displeasure with the Finger," I spewed out, admonishing the boy.

Fred shrugged his shoulders twice for okay. Then he signed his reason why he was a bit displeased.

Filled with pride, I rubbed Fred's chest.

"Aww...that's right, son. It shouldn't matter who you eat. All nationalities are equal." The boy had no head, but he sure had a big heart.

"But, daddy," Headley protested, "what about free will? Shouldn't we be able to eat who we want?"

I was so proud that we had our first round table discussion.

"Yes. But, in you and your brother's case, eating should be compromised between the both of you."

"But why, daddy?"

"Duh! Your brother doesn't have a head, so he doesn't have a mouth. He only eats what you eat."

Headley slapped his forehead. "Ugh! I keep forgetting. Sorry, daddy." Headley then rubbed his brother's shoulder. "Sorry, Fred. My bad."

Fred, in turn, held Headley's hand, rubbing it.

He went on to sign his apology for giving him the Finger and yielded to only eating bad French people.

"Aww...thanks, Fred. But that's okay, I'll eat other people, too," settled Headley.

I sighed at my two boys and glowed with pride. Appreciation seeped into my heart. Not too many fathers had conjoined twin boys with one head between both of them and who were half-zombie geniuses. My beautiful boys came away from their first round table discussion unscathed and with added maturity. Not bad for one-year-olds.

Janet entered my home, wearing a smart, navy-blue pantsuit and holding a bottle of Merlot. Fred and Headley ran up to their godmother and overwhelmed her with hugs and kisses. With tears in her eyes, Janet held the boys for a long moment. She seemed to care for them as if they were her own.

You two are growing so fast," Janet said while sighing and bending over.

Headley's face was beaming. "Daddy said that we're as big as five-year-olds."

"That's true. You boys may grow up to be basketball players."

Headley shook his head. "No, we're gonna be Wildlife Waste Handlers like our daddy. It's too important of a career to pass up."

I followed Fred's thumbs up with my own.

During dinner, Janet and I chewed away at our cheese lasagne while Mildead and the boys ate their usual faux tofu-meat aka human flesh. I knew Janet was a vegetarian; therefore, I had ordered out since Mildead didn't know how to cook anything other than meat dishes.

"Oh, Mildead, this cheese lasagne is wonderful," praised Janet with sincerity.

Headley rushed to speak as usual, "It's a take out from Mousey's restaurant."

I sent my youngest son a hard eye.

"That's a fine place. I have eaten there a couple of times," Janet replied. "By the way, what are you three eating?"

"It's tofu meat," answered Headley.

He glanced at me and smiled like he had done a good deed.

Janet grinned.

"Oh, I love tofu. Can I try some?"

"No!" Mildead and I shouted in unison.

Janet perked up, startled.

"I mean. No. There isn't any more," I lied in a much softer tone.

"But daddy, mommy has a bunch of tofu meat left." Headley pointed to a large black plastic bag on the kitchen counter.

I glared at my son who had a big brain but also a big mouth.

"No, she doesn't."

Headley folded his arms. "Yes, she does."

"Headley, no she—"

"Filmon, it's okay. This cheese lasagna is fine." interrupted Janet.

"Anyway, Janet, the tofu meat...is...not for human consumption. I mean...for regular people. It's um..."

Janet gave me an expression as though I was deliberately holding her in suspense.

"It's what, Filmon?"

" ...It's a...pres...prescription meat. Yeah."

"I never heard of prescription meat."

I struggled to continue, "Yeah, it's a...um ... a modern bio...biological systematic... a diagnostical thing in some..."

Headley rushed in for the save.

"The meat is for those mothers who have digestive problems due to having conjoined twins. The doctor had said that it was okay for Fred and me to eat the meat since we have similar gastrointestinal tracts as mommy."

"Oh, okay," said Janet, seemingly satisfied.

My son was indeed fibbing, but I gazed at him with a proud smile on my face. When Janet returned to enjoy her cheese lasagne, Headley shot me a wink and a sly grin.

During our meal, I noticed red scratch marks on the lower part of Janet's neck. I hadn't seen those marks before, so I asked her about it.

Janet whipped her hands up and covered her neck by pulling up the collar of her blouse.

"Oh, silly me. I...I'd scratched myself a week ago."

I was sceptical.

"Janet, I saw you two days ago at work, and I've never noticed those marks."

"No. I mean...yesterday..."

I knew something was wrong.

"Janet, tell me. Where did you get those scratches?"

Janet became silent as her face grew flush. I could tell that she was fighting within herself. Her green eyes were moving about and looked blank. She covered her face with her hands and then proceeded to cry.

I got up from my chair and knelt beside her.

"Janet, what's the matter?"

She shook her head as a teardrop flew off her cheek. "Nothing. I just—"

"Janet Lorraine Easley, you better tell me why you're crying?"

Janet took her hands away from her face and looked at me with her teary eyes. "My middle name isn't Lorraine. It's Marie."

"Oh, sorry.... For some reason, I thought it was Lorraine...never mind. Tell me, what's wrong?"

Janet wiped her tears from her eyes and used a dinner napkin to blow her nose.

"It was Frank. He scratched me."

"Your ex-husband?"

She managed a slight nod.

"He came by the house and said he wanted to talk.... So, I let him in. Then he began to yell...and...and he grabbed me. He started to choke me. But then, I..."

"Then you, what?"

"Then I...made a defensive maneuver and kicked him in the bazeebas. He keeled over in an instant."

"Yay, Janet!" Headley cheered, raising both arms.

I smiled. "That's a good thing, right?"

Janet returned a smile through her tears. "Yeah, it was. I called the cops, and they took him away. He spent the weekend in jail. But yesterday, he called me and threatened me, saying he was going to buy a gun and shoot me."

I felt a sudden chill, beginning to feel afraid for her. "Did you tell the cops about your ex-husband's threat?"

"Yeah. The cops had talked to him about it. But he'd denied it. I'm scared, Filmon. I believe he's really going to kill me."

I held her hands in mine. "Listen, stay over our house tonight. We'll figure something out. Okay, my dear?"

"Okay. Thank you, Filmon."

Mildead escorted Janet to the guest room upstairs while the boys and I remained at the dinner table. I felt terrible for Janet, but I also felt pissed off at her ex-husband who was an overbearing bully, especially when drunk. I had met him several times over the years, and each time he had made me very uncomfortable. And I'm sure there were other occasions when he had abused Janet. I was heated as my mind was spinning.

Fred tapped the table then signed something that I didn't fully catch. I was too engrossed, thinking about Janet's ex.

"Wh...what was that, son?" I asked, finally coming out of my dark reverie.

Fred signed again.

"Oh, what am I thinking about? I...I'm just mad at Janet's ex-husband."

"Yeah, we are, too," said Headley. "Daddy, Frank's a bad guy, huh?"

"Yes, he is, son."

"Is he French?"

"Um...I don't know. He may... hey, what are you getting at?"

Headley had a Mona Lisa smile, but then it slowly turned into a wicked grin. "Let's eat the sucker, daddy."

Fred threw up two enthusiastic thumbs.

I had to think about that one. But not that long. "Let's run it by your mother first."

Headley's big black eyes circled the room.

"Daddy, mommy's a zombie. She won't care."

"Hey, we're a family. Before we eat anyone's brain, we have to plan it first...as a family."

Headley perked up and grinned. "Daddy, you're gonna eat brains, too?"

"Oh, heck no. You guys are the zombies. I'll be the getaway driver or something."

Headley was right, Mildead hadn't cared when I had suggested to her that we eat Janet's ex. In fact, she had loved the idea. The next morning, I asked Janet, in a roundabout way, where her ex lived.

She'd told me that he lived in a studio apartment downtown, across the street from the public library. I wasn't too optimistic about that—apartments had too many people living nearby. I needed to case the joint first.

The following day, I drove downtown and pulled up in front of the only apartment building that was across the street from the library. It was a run-down brick building with four floors and two rickety fire escapes.

I got out of the Pacer and walked over to the entrance of the apartment building, where I browsed through a directory that was covered by a plate of glass. I wasn't sure if Janet's last name Easley was also Frank's surname. I went on, checking for the name Easley, without any luck.

Then I checked for the first names that had an initial of F for Frank. Three names had an F before their surnames—an F. Wang, F. Gomez, and F.Harrison. I had met Frank before. Thus I ruled out Wang and Gomez. But just to be sure, I rang F.Harrison's doorbell.

A scruffy voice came on the intercom.

"Yeah, who is it?'

I used my Elvis voice as cover. " 'Scuse me, is ya name Frank, baby?"

"Yeah. Who is this?"

"Ya...ya have an ex-wife named Janet?"

"That's right. Now who in the hell is this?"

"Never mind that, baby. Thank ya very much." The right apartment. The right man.

The next evening, my little zombie family and I went into action. We arrived downtown after midnight. It was somewhat chilly outside and quiet—an excellent night to cleanse wickedness from the world. I parked the Pacer around the corner from the apartment building and led my family to the entrance. We checked the surroundings for movement of any kind. Nothing. Then Headley went to work.

"This is so exciting, daddy. It's our first manhunt as a family," Headley said.

"Are you sure you can open the door?" There was a tinge of nervousness in my voice.

"I'm pretty sure, daddy. Now stand back and keep a lookout." Headley reached into the front pocket of his little bell-bottom jeans and took out two hairpins as Fred tiptoed in front of the entrance door. Headley then inserted the two pins into the door's lock, while humming the Mission Impossible theme song. Within two minutes, the entrance door clicked open.

"Voila."

I gave my son a proud grin and turned to Mildead. "It's good to have genius boys."

Mildead smiled and winked. As we all entered the foyer, I asked Headley, "Son, where did you learn how to pick a lock?"

"The internet."

"Sweet."

We got out of the elevator on the fourth level, and soft stepped it toward room 411. There were fifteen other rooms on the floor as a brown carpet paved our way. Room 411 was at the end of the hallway near a rear stairwell. The door to each room was red, and the walls were the colour of brass.

As we passed through the hallway, nervousness and excitement stirred up inside me. I believed we were doing the right thing by getting rid of an abuser of women. We were doing it for my friend Janet and for the women who would have crossed Frank's path in the future. He was a bad man, and my family were good people—albeit zombies.

We brought ourselves outside of Frank's apartment. Fred and Headley wanted to knock on the door, so they fronted Mildead and me, ready for action. Before tapping the door, they checked to see if the hallway was clear. With no one in sight, my sons, at the same time, knocked a shave-and-a-haircut ten cents tune on the door, then another. Finally, we heard mumbling and heavy footsteps inside the apartment. The door swung open, and

Frank appeared with a pissed-off look on his face. The first person he saw was me.

"I know you. You're Janet's friend. What the hell do you want at this hour?" Frank snarled.

I greeted Janet's ex, showing a warm smile. "Hello, Frank. Meet my lovely family."

Frank peered at Mildead, and then he laid his eyes down on Fred and Headley.

"Ugh! What the hell is that little thing?"

Headley looked up at Frank and said with a charming grin, "Hi, I'm Headley. And this is my brother Fred. Are you French?"

The disgust on Frank's face turned to confusion. "Wha.... What? Yeah.... I'm French, on my mother's side. What about it?"

"Cool!"

A short time later, we stuffed the uneaten parts of Frank's body in a plastic garbage bag as a take out.

Getting rid of Janet's ex was bittersweet. On the one hand, I'd felt exhilarated that there was one less woman beater in the world, and my little zombie family had gotten a nice meal out of it, too. But we did take the law in our own hands—and that indeed bothered me. When we arrived home, I told my family that I wanted to be alone for a while. It was 2:12 in the morning, and I sat out front on the porch swing, mulling over if what we had just done was an act of heroism or just plain murder. At 2:13 am, I decided that it was heroism. I slept like a baby that night.

Four days passed by and Janet called me from her home to say that she'd filed a restraining order on her ex. But when the sheriff had gone over to Frank's apartment to serve him the papers, the door had been left ajar, and the condo had the look of being ransacked. Also, Frank hadn't shown up for work in the past three days. Yet the best part, Janet had said, the police had listed Frank as a missing person. Janet had been happy. It was probably the best phone call that I have ever had. My family's act of heroism had given my friend happiness and a sense of peace. Janet's feeling of joy had been the validation that I'd needed to go on rounding up bad people and sentencing them to death by a zombie. It felt good to be a hero.

Following our emotional goodbyes to Janet, my little family and I were on the road in my Pacer, heading west toward California. My mother had once said that there was plenty of riffraff out west, particularly in Los Angeles. I also had remembered her saying, "Pfft...city of angels, my butt. What a country-dixon!" My mother surely had a way with words. I suddenly recalled that I have a nephew there, my brother Zeke's kid from a previous marriage. I haven't seen the boy in fifteen years. Therefore, Los Angeles was my zombie family's destination to visit relatives. But more importantly, to kick some Country-Dixons' butts. Or eat them, whichever came first.

CHAPTER 9

The Zombie Crusades

WE STOPPED IN FORT WORTH, Texas, for a short time to eat. Soon we were back on highway 20, planning to connect to Highway 10, then it would be clear sailing to California. However, driving through Texas was akin to waiting in line with my mother for women's restroom at a Major League baseball game. It took forever. Yet that's when I'd learned the ingenious concept of sitting and peeing.

Cleaner toilet seats, cleaner bathroom floors. I never stood and peed again. Maybe I could learn another ingenious concept while I drove through this big fat southern state.

While Mildead and the boys were thinking zombie thoughts, probably brain-eating, I took the time to see the sights of Texas as I drove, hoping to also come up with new and innovative ideas.

Whenever I was impatient, I've often learned something new. Impatience and genius often went hand in hand. When we passed the city of Abilene, a thought came into my head, which happened every once in a while. What if I became a zombie, too? I'd never had to worry about dying. Unless someone shot me in the head or something, moreover, I wouldn't have to spend any money on groceries or sleeping aids.

Though mostly, my zombie family would undoubtedly love it if I joined their little undead club.

I'd just have Mildead eat some part of me. A little piece of me, of course. Some part of my body where there wasn't too much blood, minimising the pain. My impatient genius mind went to work: Mildead could eat my pinky finger. Nah, I need to drink tea. Hmm, I could have her eat my other pinky, but I use that one to clean out my ear. Lemme see... what part of my body do I rarely use?

Hmm. Ha! I almost said to myself, brain. Wait! Do I need my brain? Yeah, I need it. Never mind that one. My brain would be the last thing I'd part with. Wait! That's a lie. It would be my little winky.

Pfff...I'd rather have my little winky than my brain any day...duh.

Okay, I wonder if she ate my hair, would it turn me into a zombie? Nah, that wouldn't work. That would be ideal, though. Not much pain there nor blood for that matter. Unless she yanked my hair outta my skull. Ugh! I shuddered at that thought. How about my left butt cheek? Nah, then I'd be sitting with a slanted posture—too uncomfortable. After a few more ingenious ideas wafted inside my head, I soon came to realise that maybe I didn't want to become a zombie after all. Perhaps another time.

I loved pizza and ice cream too much to become one of the living dead right now.

We finally made it out of Texas, and then we connected to highway 10, driving through New Mexico, on the left lane, doing a top speed of 52 miles per hour. I wanted to get to California as soon as possible; my little family was hungry. Unfortunately, a highway patrol car flashed its lights, inducing us to pull over. It wasn't long before a husky highway patrolman tapped on the driver's side window. I struggled to roll down the window only a few inches, for it stuck badly, and it was filthy from the long drive. Only my eyes and eyeglasses were visible to the officer.

The Highway patrolman gestured for me to roll down the window all the way.

"I'm sorry, officer. But my window is stuck," I said regretfully.

"Then exit from the vehicle, sir," the highway patrolman ordered.

"Um.... What's the problem, officer?"

"Just exit the vehicle."

I was irritated, but I obeyed by getting out of the car. I stood several feet from the officer and leaned my arm on top of the car door, which I'd left open.

The highway patrolman gave me the once over, seemingly suspicious. But all police officers were suspicious when they stopped someone. He then glanced into the car and laid his eyes on Mildead who returned a slight smile. He was about to check the backseat, where Fred and Headley were, but I stole his attention.

"Was I speeding, officer?"

The highway patrolman curled his upper lip. "Speeding? You were on the fast lane, driving only 54 miles per hour. And the speed limit is 65. You should have been on the far right—"

"Aha!" I said, raising my voice and pointing a finger. "I was doing 52 miles per hour! My car can't go over 52. You police are always exaggerating to give out more tickets."

"Sir, you were going too slow, holding up traffic. You didn't notice cars passing you up and the drivers honking at you?"

My eyes narrowed at the officer's mirrored sunglasses. "I thought they were just honking greetings, so I kept honking back."

The highway patrolman shook his head.

"Driver's license, proof of insurance, and registration, please." He then took his sunglasses off to get a better look at my boys.

It took me less than a minute to provide all the documents.

"I'm sorry, officer. But I didn't know I was going too slow. I thought I was really movin'."

The officer rolled his eyes before examining my drivers' license. Then he stepped back a few feet, near the rear car-window, and called me over to him by jerking his head.

"Look here," he said, lowering his voice. "I'm going to give you a break. Instead of me giving you an expensive ticket or possibly arresting you for reckless driving, you can pay the fine in cash, half price, right now, making it easier for both of us."

I hated getting tickets, but I appreciated getting breaks.

"Okay, officer. How much is the"

"Daddy, don't give him any money! That's illegal!"
Headley's voice was stern. His head and Fred's upper
body were sticking out of the passenger car window.

The highway patrolman was shocked at the sight of
my boys. His instincts caused him to draw his revolver,
pointing it at Fred and Headley.

"Damn! What in the name of Mary Shelley is that!"

"Hey, don't point that gun at them!" I yelled. "They're
my sons!"

My fatherly instincts suddenly took control over me.
I pounced on the officer, tackling him to the ground. The
officer's revolver flew out of his hand and landed near the
front tire of my car. I managed to crawl on top of the officer, straddling him. I held onto his neck, holding him
down with my left hand.

Then I raised my clenched right fist and growled.
"Never point a gun at my boys! They're only a year old, for
goodness sakes!"

"We're one and a half, daddy!" Headley cried out, as
he and Fred were getting out from the car.

Fred threw out quick hand gestures.

"And Fred says, knock his block off, daddy! But leave
the brain!"

I turned my head and yelled at my kids. "Hey, get back
in the car!"

Before I returned my attention to the highway patrolman, he twisted his body, causing me to roll with him, and he ended up on top of me. The next thing I saw was his fist flying toward my face.

Then came darkness.

I woke up with a sore, swollen cheek. I was sitting in the front seat of the Pacer, not knowing how much time had elapsed.

We were still parked on the side of the highway while Mildead and the boys were at their usual seating positions in the car.

Dazed and groggy, I rubbed my sore cheek and turned to the side, eyeing Mildead picking her dentures with a toothpick.

"Mommy, pass the Baby Wipes, please," said Headley, holding his hands up like he was a doctor in the ER, before surgery.

Mildead reached down next to her left foot and picked up a plastic container of Baby Wipes. She pulled out a few sheets, handing them to Headley.

"Thank you, mommy."

Headley let out a loud burp, and Fred followed with a resounding fart.

"Oops, excuse us... Yum, that was good."

Fred rubbed his full tummy and used his other hand to give Headley a thumbs up.

As my head was clearing, I scanned the surroundings for the highway patrolman. I couldn't find him nor his patrol car.

"Hey, guys, where's the officer?

After Headley wiped his mouth, he replied.

"Oh, you won't see him anymore."

Fred signed a retort.

Headley giggled. "Yeah, nor his brain."

I had a good feeling about what may have happened but wasn't surprised.

"What about his patrol car?"

"Oh, mommy drove it down the embankment, out of sight, after Fred had dismantled its video capabilities."

I exhaled a deep sigh. "I am so proud of you guys.... All right, group hug..."

As soon as we broke out of our little family embrace, Headley said.

"Hey, daddy...guess what the name of that dirty cop was?"

"What?"

Headley opened his hand and showed me a small, gold-plated name tag which read. "French."

A wide grin showed on my face. "That's destiny! Vive la France, baby!"

"Oui oui, daddy!" Headley burped, and Fred farted again. "Excuse us."

Mildead and I looked at each other then cracked up, laughing. I promptly started up the Pacer and drove it back on the highway, heading due west. In the far right lane, of course.

Soon darkness fell upon us, and I was getting too sleepy to drive. Mildead volunteered to drive, but I declined her offer, for I didn't want to end up in Canada again. Instead of sleeping at a rest stop, I decided to treat my little family to a night's stay at a cozy Motel 6, which was coming up at the next exit.

In a short time, we checked in to room 11, where two double beds awaited. Before I readied myself to bed, Headley asked me about my father.

"Daddy, you never talk much about our grandpa. All Fred and I know is that grandpa ran away with a gay Bollywood star when you were ten."

Headley paused to read Fred's signing. "Oh, yeah.

And that he was a feisty Italian."

"Let me tuck you boys in first before I tell you what I know about your grandpa."

I unfolded the bedding and laid out two pillows in T-formation at the top of the bed while Fred and Headley changed into their Zombie Man, buttoned-top pyjamas. Anxious to hear about their grandpa, Fred and Headley hopped in bed, ready to listen to the story. I sighed and smiled at my boys' cuteness.

"Okay, the night before your grandpa ran off with Rakesh, the gay Bollywood star, he'd told me that we were descendants of a prominent Italian family, Troutawini."

"Huh? Trout...awini? Ha! Ha! That's a funny name, daddy, sounds like a trout's weeny.

Headley joked, laughing. Fred broke out in silent laughter, as his shoulders shook hard.

I frowned. "Hey, don't make fun. You boys are Trout-awinis, too."

The laughter grew louder when Mildead, who was lying down on the other bed, joined the laugh brigade.

"Okay. Okay. You guys wanna hear the story or not?"

Headley's laughter died down to a smile. "Sorry, daddy. Let's hear the story... Hey, why did grandpa shorten the name?"

"He didn't. His grandfather shortened it, so silly Americans like you wouldn't make fun of it."

"Oh...sorry, daddy."

I checked around for smiles on the verge of laughter or shaking shoulders before I continued.

"Your grandpa had told me that the Troutawini name was prominent but also notorious throughout all of Italy. Many of your ancestors were angry, vindictive people, and always looking for a fight. They—"

"Why were they angry, daddy?" asked Headley.

"Because of the secret that all of Italy knows but refuse to share with the world."

"What secret?"

I loomed closer to my sons, widening my eyes. "...That your ancestor, Bastardo Troutawini, was the true master of the Mona Lisa."

Headley's mouth gaped. "No way, daddy."

"Yes, way."

"But I thought Leonardo da Vin—"

"Quiet!"

The harshness of my voice startled the boys.

"We are never to say that name. For the ghost of Bastardo, Troutawini will haunt you while you sleep."

"I don't believe in ghosts, daddy," uttered Headley with an assured tone.

I'd forgotten Headley didn't believe in ghost, so I added something that he was afraid of, "Then, an Italian clown will haunt your little butt!"

Headley screamed.

What is it with that boy and clowns, I thought. I leaned over and kissed Headley on the forehead.

"I'm sorry, son, for scaring you. But this is a serious family business. Just never say, Leonardo da Vinci.

"Okay?"

Headley gasped, taking in loads of air and then breathed out. "Daddy, you...you said the name.

"Dammit, I know!" I proceeded to cross myself with that Catholic manoeuvre, and then I chanted five Hail Marys.

"I didn't know you were Catholic, daddy."

"I'm not. But it seems to work in scary movies."

Fred and Headley crossed themselves with speedy fingers, but their crosses were more like triangles.

"Okay. Where was I?"

"You said our ancestor Bastardo Troutawini was the true master of the Mona Lisa," answered Headley, as his eyes were nearly popping out.

"Oh, yeah. The true master of the Mona Lisa..."

* * *

Bastardo Troutawini was born over 500 years ago in the town of Vinci, within the region of Florence, Italy. He worked in waste management as a Bucket Collector, an esteemed job position, he had often boasted. His duty was to collect buckets of human waste throughout Vinci and dump the contents in the Arno river. Although he had loved his job immensely, his real passion was painting. He would paint anything that inspired him.

Bastardo's best friend was the great Leonardo da Vinci, who was a master artist at the time, among other things. Both men were deeply in love with the same beautiful woman. And her name was Mona Lisa. But Bastardo had no idea that his best friend was also in love with her. He had always thought that Leonardo favoured young men. Bastardo would later find out that his famous best friend had in fact loved both men and women.

One day, Bastardo finished a portrait of Mona Lisa, strictly from memory. A fantastic feat for any artist. He then visited his best friend's home and allowed Leonardo to gaze upon the portrait.

"Bastardo, you call that a painting? It looks just like your mama. Ha, I laugh at you!" Leonardo's words pierced Bastardo's heart.

He had respected Leonardo, believing anything his friend had said. Doubt and humiliation seeped in his soul. "I was a going to present the portrait to Mona Lisa...as a gift. But a...now I'm a not so sure."

"Forgetta 'bout that a portrait. I will show you a better painting. Don't move," said Leonardo, who then left Bastardo wallowing in his own uncertainty as an artist. He soon returned with a painting, covered in a white sheet.

"Now, this is a masterpiece!" Leonardo unveiled a painting of two pairs of dogs sitting at a table, playing two games of chess.

"This is art imitating life, my friend."

Bastardo was amazed at the sight of his friend's painting. "It is truly a masterpiece, Leonardo. You had captured the true essence of your neighbour Carlo's dogs.

My portrait of Mona Lisa does not compare to yours. I will destroy my painting."

Bastardo lifted his portrait above his head.

"No!" shouted Leonardo. "Don't destroy it.... Since I'm your best friend, I will give you my painting of Carlo's dogs, so you could present it to the lovely Mona Lisa. And you will give me your portrait of Mona Lisa, and I will probably hang it over my toilet. No use wasting it, eh? Art is art."

"But...Leonardo that is too generous. I—"

"Not another word. We are best friends, yes?"

Bastardo nodded. He never loved his friend more than that moment.

The following evening, an excited Bastardo visited Mona Lisa at her home, and he presented the painting of the dogs to her.

Mona Lisa was deeply insulted. "What is this? You give me a painting of dogs! You think I'm a dog, eh!"

"Mona Lisa, no! I don't think you a dog. You are a beaut—"

Mona Lisa slapped Bastardo's face, and then she pointed to the front door. "Leave a my house, you a pig of a man!"

Bastardo was dumbfounded and internally devastated. But before he turned to leave her home, he froze, shocked from what his eyes were seeing. The portrait of his Mona Lisa was hanging over her fireplace.

The next day, Bastardo was thrown in prison for nearly strangling his best friend to death. He was given the harshest sentence possible: thirty years. To the people of Vinci, it was an unforgivable act for someone to put their hands on the living legend, Leonardo da Vinci. After his sentencing, Bastardo had the look of a mad man, filled with rage.

"Leonardo is a thief!" Bastardo cried out, piercing the air with his voice. "He is the one who should be in prison!"

The people of Vinci were appalled of Bastardo's outburst. They hissed at him, as he was being taken away.

"I am more superior artist than Leonardo, that thief of love and art!" yelled Bastardo. "I...Bastardo Travolta Isabella Rosalini Troutawini is the true master of the Mona Lisa!"

***

"What a story, daddy," said Headley. "Is it really true?"

I gazed into my son's eyes and replied. "Hey, who ya gonna believe? Grandpa Troutawini or some history book?"

Fred and Headley raised their arms. "Grandpa!"

"Good boys."

Zombie Sisters Stick Together

SODEAD AND TOODEAD STOOD in the shadows, outside an avocado-green house, where nary a light was lit. The twin sisters had an uncontrollable urge to be with their sister Mildead. It was an inherent desire that was nearly as strong as their hunger for human flesh. They needed to get their sister back by any means necessary, yet there was one obstacle: Filmon Trout. The sisters believed that if he were out of the way, then Mildead would surely return to them.

"We must get that pesky, skinny man alone, away from Mildead and our nephews," murmured Toodead, as she held her gaze at Filmon's home.

"Yes. I'll distract Mildead and the boys while you feast on Filmon. But save me some of his brains," said Sodead.

Toodead smirked. "Maybe just a small portion...Wait—" A light was turned on in the living room. "I saw a woman who just passed near the front window, but it wasn't Mildead."

"Hmm...come, let's make inquiries."

"After you, my dear sister."

Sodead and Toodead held hands while they sauntered up the stairs of the two-storey home. Upon reaching the front porch, the sisters heard a stereo playing an orchestrated version of Beethoven's Fur Elise, from inside the house. Sodead rang the doorbell twice before the front door opened seconds later.

"Hello, ladies. May I help you?" welcomed Janet grinning.

Sodead barely cracked a smile. "Is Mildead or Filmon at home?"

Janet was a bit irked for not receiving a reciprocated greeting.

"I'm sorry, they're away indefinitely. They took the boys on a trip. I'm Janet, a friend of Filmon's. I'm house-sitting."

Both sisters pushed out an exasperating sigh. Then Sodead asked,

"Where did they go?"

Janet became even more irritated—they still hadn't introduced themselves. Maybe their bad manners were due to their sickly appearance, she thought.

"Excuse me, who are you?"

Toodead pushed forward, brushing back her sister. "I'm Toodead, and this is Sodead. We're Mildead's sisters."

Janet instantly showed the sisters another welcoming smile. "Why didn't you say that in the first place. Come...come in."

Janet led Sodead and Toodead to the living room, thinking they resembled Mildead, in every which way—that pale to nearly greenish skin colour, skinny physique, and that look of hunger as if they hadn't eaten in a month. Janet pointed to the sofa, gesturing for the sisters to take a seat.

"Would you both like some coffee or tea?" Janet politely offered.

"So, it's just you here...house-sitting?" Sodead asked with roaming eyes.

Janet's irritation returned—her hospitality was slighted. "That's right. It's just me. Would you like coffee or—"

"Where did Mildead and Filmon go?" continued Sodead.

Janet emitted a low-decibel harrumph sound, forgoing the hospitality of offering the sisters any refreshments. She instead sat down on Filmon's recliner. "They went to Los Angeles weeks ago."

Toodead sputtered. "Do you have an address?"

"No, I don't. But Filmon did mention that he had a relative living in Compton, a city in the Los Angeles area.... Why? Is there something wrong?"

"No. Nothing's wrong. We're just anxious to see our sister, and maybe a...little hungry," admitted Sodead, who suddenly hit Janet with a wink of an eye. "I bet you have a tasty brain."

Janet jerked up and sat on the edge of the recliner. "Tasty what?"

Sodead and Toodead stood up from the sofa, their eyes fixed ominously on Janet's confused countenance. The twin sisters then growled in unison.

"Brain!"

A violent struggle ensued, with bodies hitting the floor. The sounds of moans and groans ascended to harrowing screams that resonated throughout the house. Blood splattered. Windows shattered. Clothes ripped. Feet slipped. Paintings fell. Faces swelled. Furniture broke. Necks choked. Fists unclenched. Then came silence.

The front door creaked open, and the sisters appeared, bruised and beaten. Behind them was a pissed-off Janet, who in the next instance, kicked each sister in the ass like she was punting a football.

One by one, Sodead and Toodead tumbled off the front porch and down the stairs, crashing on the sidewalk. Each sister struggled to pick themselves up and limped off toward the street while Janet stood with fists on hips at the top of the stairs, posing like a superhero.

Sodead turned to her sister as they crossed the street and uttered, "I thought that lady was bluffing when she'd said that she was a 5th-degree black belt in karate."

"Oh, forget about it. Let's go find a dog to eat."

"Yeah. A small one."

Police sirens sounded off nearby, prompting Sodead and Toodead to cut around the corner, ducking out in an alleyway. From behind a small backyard fence, a light-brown chihuahua howled in the darkness, harmonising terribly with the police sirens. Within a minute, the howling ceased, and the poor, unwitting chihuahua was no more.

Toodead licked the chihuahua's blood off her fingers then said. "That little brat of a dog was better than nothing."

Sodead frowned, showing an unsatisfactory expression. "But I need to munch on some human brain before I go mad."

"Don't worry, my dear sister. We'll have the human brain very soon. We'll feast on the first human who picks us up."

"Picks us up?"

"Yes. While we're hitchhiking to Los Angeles."

Sodead twisted a sinister smile.

"Excellent."

The early morning sun brought a comforting smile to James T. Fenimore, who was driving his dark-blue van for an hour and a half, searching for a suitable place to dump a dead body. One couldn't drop a fresh corpse just anywhere, he thought. A wooded area, away from pedestrian paths was a good place as any. Or better yet, a river. Although his favourite place to dump dead bodies had been at a shabby cemetery called Mac and Donald's Burial World, which had no security. He had chosen gravesites away from the street, dug them up, and set his freshly killed victims atop the lifeless occupants.

Though lately, Mac and Donald's Burial World had been bustling with late night activity, putting a halt to his body dumping. Damn kids or squatters, James said to himself. There were three types of people he hated the most: loose women, reality TV stars, and gay astronauts from the ghetto. The types of people who had been his victims and who he'd subconsciously desired the most or to become. James Thomas Fenimore was a serial killer. He had taken the lives of seventeen young men and women, and he was far from done.

On this particular morning, the warmth of the morning sun set off a recent memory that gave him chills and excitement. A memory of his murderous act of bludgeoning to death a young female stripper. A burly man in his early 30's, James held the van's steering wheel at the 10-2 position, with abnormally large hands due to his six foot, six inch frame and a seven year drug habit, shooting up crystal meth. A dark, bushy beard made him look ten years older and like a hillbilly miner from West Virginia.

He glanced at the rearview mirror and adjusted its setting, then he inadvertently caught his own gaze that lasted no more than two seconds. His blue eyes were sad looking, but they didn't reflect his mood, which was the feeling of satisfaction, surrounded by a thin layer of bliss. He often felt this way after a kill that went smoothly, on top of a shot of crystal meth in his vein. He was a working drug addict—his addiction rarely interfered with his extra-curricular activities.

James was a cautious driver—serial killers normally were. Getting stopped by police for a traffic violation could be fatal, and what was also a rookie mistake was dumping dead bodies in daylight, so he decided to head back home and wait for darkness. After James made a u-turn near afreeway entrance, he suddenly pressed hard on the brakes, screeching to a stop. On the side of the road were two sexy women hitchhiking. One held a cardboard sign that read Los Angeles. He knew he shouldn't have stopped—there was a dead body in the back of his van. Yet his uncontrollable urge to satisfy his most inner desire overtook his sensibilities.

"Hello there, ladies." James greeted the ladies after Toodead opened the passenger door.

"Hi, cutie pie. Are you going anywhere near Los Angeles?" Toodead asked.

"Possibly, if the company is fun," James winked.

Sodead pushed her way past her sister and boldly sat in the front seat.

"Oh, we're fun and certainly not boring."

James felt an odd sensation in his gut. The two women were attractive but sickly looking at the same time. These were definitely loose women, he said to himself. But he didn't seem to have that feeling of the upper hand, which he usually felt after picking up his prey. His first instinct was to drive off without them, and yet, he was a slave to intrigue and desire.

"My name is J.T."

Sodead introduced herself, as Toodead sat on a crate that was in between the front bucket seats.

Their sharp zombie sense of smell instantly detected the unmistakable odour of death. They knew right away that the man wasn't one of their own, and then they brought their attention to the back of the van.

"What do you have back there, J.T.? I smell something odd but delightful," Toodead said.

James was caught off guard. "Huh? What smell?"

Sodead hit James with a cold glance. "Like the smell of death."

"Oh...uh...it's a deer I had hit on the road. I didn't want to leave it there, so I...I just took it with me...and uh, placed it in the back."

Toodead rose eagerly from the crate and said, "Ooh, let me check it out."

"No!" James's voice was high-pitched and piercing, then it lowered, "It...it may have some kind of disease." He reached over and grabbed Toodead's arm and made her sit back down.

Sodead shot James a suspicious glare.

"It's not a deer, J.T. Is it?"

Although James was a cold-hearted killer and twice as big and strong as the two women, he felt like a little kid who had been caught stealing a candy bar.

"Uh...what do you—"

"It's a dead human body, huh? We know the difference between the odour of a dead animal and a dead human, J.T.," said Sodead with an eerie tone.

James gave Toodead and Sodead curious glances. He could not figure them out. Part of him wanted to slash their throats, and the other part of him wanted to get to know them, for he was certainly intrigued by their presence and behavior. He decided to stay in character and kill them.

"I need to pull over, ladies. I...I need to get something from the back," said James.

"You haven't answered my question." Sodead's voice was firm.

"I will as soon as I stop the van."

James veered off the right lane and parked the van on an embankment. He unbuckled his seat belt and bent down to the left side of his seat. He snapped back up with a large, 12-inch hunting knife in his hand, waving the blade in a threatening manner.

"Yes. It is a dead body."

"Wait, J.T. Was it your plan to pick us up and kill us?" Toodead asked calmly.

James' eyes widened to an evil-looking glare.

"That's right. It was my plan. Now…"

Toodead turned to Sodead, and then both sisters suddenly broke out laughing.

The confusion caused James to stutter.

"Wh…what's so…so funny?"

"Hey, we…we were going to kill you, too!" Toodead cried out between laughter.

"And, eat your brain!" followed Sodead who kept up her cackling.

James seemed more confused. "Eat my brain?"

Sodead calmed down to a chuckle. "Yeah…we're zombies."

James became silent from disbelief. Then he raised his voice, "Gimme a break. You two aren't zombies."

Toodead put out her left arm toward James. "It's true. Check my pulse."

James placed his large thumb on Toodead's wrist. "You're cold."

Toodead twisted the corner of her mouth. "I'm dead."

James continued to check Toodead's pulse.

"My god…you don't have a pulse." He reached over Toodead and snatched Sodead's wrist. Cold and no pulse. The serial killer in James raced from disbelief then slowly took a turn to intuition. "I knew there was something different about you two!"

Right after his comment, James accidentally nicked himself on the side of his cheek with his hunting knife, drawing blood. He wiped his cheek with his fingers and stared at the smeared blood, trickling down onto his palm.

Toodead and Sodead pointed their fingers at James and once again laughed out loud.

James responded by joining in the laughter.

The good-time moment gradually died down. All three killers felt a stand-off might be compromised to a possible truce.

"So, are you two still going to eat me?" said James half-jokingly.

Toodead eyes hit a peripheral wall, scoping her prey or her killer. "Are you still going to kill us?"

"Actually, no. I'm beginning to like you girls."

"And I like you." Toodead then turned to her sister. "What about you, my dear?"

Sodead frowned. "I was hoping for brain."

James perked up, smiling. "You know, I gotta fresh, dead young woman in the back of the van. You're welcome to her brain."

Sodead instantly cheered up. "Yes, I like him!"

The two sisters didn't waste any time moving to the back of the van and munching on the dead woman's brain. James swiveled his body around in his seat and was amazed by what he saw. The sight of Toodead and Sodead savagely ripping apart and devouring a human brain excited him nearly as much as killing his victims. It made him want to kill again, and also, to see more of the sisters' eating frenzy. The dinner party ended a short time later, then Toodead and Sodead drifted back to their seats at the front of the van.

"Thank you, J.T. That brain was indeed delicious. I'm so full," said Toodead, holding her stomach.

"Yeah. Thanks, man," added Sodead, sucking her teeth.

James nodded and said. "You ladies are very welcome," then he took out several napkins from his pocket and offered them to the sisters. "By the way, why are you both going to Los Angeles?"

"We need to get our older sister back. She's there with her dumb boyfriend and their two kids," Toodead divulged.

James stroked his beard before he spoke again, "Well, I don't have any pressing needs to attend. I could drive you both there, no problem."

Toodead gave James a grateful smile. "That's wonderful. Thank you."

"Hey, maybe we could pick up hitchhikers on the way," James said, lifting his eyebrows twice.

"Yeah, let's go," agreed a game Sodead.

James offered his hand to the sisters. "Partners?"

One after the other Toodead and Sodead shook James' massive hand, and one after the other they both said, "partners," respectively.

CHAPTER 11

City of Angels—A Country-Dixon

"THERE IT IS BOYS, Los Angeles," I proclaimed, moving my eyes from side to side, admiring the vastness of the city's landscape of multiple freeways and a myriad of cars with only one person in them.

"Where, daddy? I can't see through the fog," Headley uttered, squinting.

"Oh, that's not fog, son. That's smog. You see how the smog blends perfectly with the crusty brown mountains," I mused. "You know, it's quite breathtaking."

"Daddy, you mean the smog takes your breath away."

I glanced at Headley through the rearview mirror and chuckled. Good one, son."

Fred threw up hand shapes and flicking fingers.

"Daddy, Fred asked if we could go to Hollywood...see some movie stars."

"Sure. But first we'll have to stop and see your cousin."

Headley grinned with excitement. "We have a cousin here?"

I turned briefly for a fraction of a second. "I didn't tell you guys?"

Headley shook his head, and Fred wagged a finger.

"Yeah, he lives in Compton, with his mother, uncle Zeke's first wife."

"Compton?" Headley said.

"Compton is one of many small cities in the Los Angeles area."

"Oh, okay.... So, our cousin is uncle Zeke's son."

"Yep."

"What's his name?"

"Winston.... Hey, and guess what," I said with a sly grin.

"What, daddy?"

"Your cousin Winston is half black."

Headley's eyes popped wide open. "Really?"

I nodded. "Uh huh."

"Cool!" Headley raised a fist. "We all black, daddy."

I smiled. "That's right, son. We all black."

My older brother Zeke was nine years my senior. At nineteen, he had married his high-school sweetheart who happened to be African American. Her name was Gloria. Nine months later, Winston Huey Newton Trout was born. The first years of their marriage had been great, but like a lot of marriages, the love had soured, and divorce soon followed. Zeke had stayed in Ohio and Gloria had taken off with their son to live with relatives in Compton, a city known for its notorious African American gangs, the Crips and Bloods, who were deadly rivals, dealing in the lucrative drug trade and committing a vast amount of crimes.

Crip gang members wore predominantly blue clothing, and sometimes rags (street name for bandanas), which were folded around their foreheads or hanging from their pants pockets. Blood gang members sported red clothing and red rags. Anyone who wore the Blood colours in Crip neighbourhoods was in danger of getting beat up or shot, and vice versa in Blood neighbourhoods. Each member in either gang used hand signs, a form of sign language, to flash their allegiance, and an important tool for communicating in and out of jails and prisons.

I aimed the Pacer toward the east side of Compton on Alondra blvd., and we ended up at the address that My brother Zeke had given me, a modest single-story home, with a four-foot-high chainlink fence surrounding a small garden in the front yard. On the front porch, were four thug-looking African American men, all dressed in white wife-beater t-shirts, blue jeans, and blue bandanas around their heads. Two of the younger men were drinking their own 40-ounce bottle of beer, and the older two were sharing a blunt, a hollowed out cigar, filled with marijuana.

"Look, daddy, our people," Headley excitedly crooned, pointing toward the men.

I got a kick out of my son and his infatuation with the African American side of our family, even though the boy is white as a snowflake in December. "All right, nice. They look like they're enjoying their Saturday."

"It's Tuesday, daddy."

"Oh. Oh, yeah.... Okay, stay here. Let me ask them if your cousin Winston still lives at this address."

I stepped out of the car and adjusted my red and gold San Francisco 49er cap, then I tucked in my bright-red t-shirt inside the waistline of my pants. Although I was dressed casual, I still wanted to look neat and presentable whenever I was about to meet new people. As I made my way toward the house, all four men slowly raised themselves from their perch and reached inside their waistbands.

I waved a greeting before I mouthed off.

"Hello, gentlemen. I'm Filmon Trout."

All four men gravitated my way and surrounded me. The tallest and oldest of the four, a muscular behemoth of a man, snarled. "You got balls, white boy. Comin' in our 'hood wearin' dose colours."

I was going to mention that my ancestor was a black slave, but I saved that information for a later time.

"Colours?"

"The red shirt on yo' back and da red cap on yo' head. And, to add even mo' disrespect to us, ya wearin' a 'Frisco cap in L.A."

"Hell nah. A 'Frisco cap? Lemme smoke dis fool," said a younger man who reached deeper into his waistband, and who was so black, shades of purple invaded his skin.

"Hold up," the muscular man said without taking his eyes off of me. Then he sneered, "What you here fo, white boy?"

I hesitated my answer because I was still a bit confused about their animosity toward my attire.

"Oh. I...I was wondering if Winston Trout still lives here?"

The black/purple young man spat back a quick reply, "Who dat? Dey ain't no Win—"

"Dat's Lil' Smokey, cuz," the muscular man said to his homie.

"Lil' Smokey name, Winston?" smirked the black/purple youth.

I pressed my way back into the conversation. "Oh, you guys know Winston? Does he still live here?"

The muscular man gave me a suspicious eye. "Yeah. He my stepson. What you want wit him?"

My face glowed like a kid eating ice cream. "Hey, he my nephew! I mean...he's my nephew.

"Winston's my brother Zeke's son. By the way, what's your name? We're sort of related."

"My name's G-Killa. And don't get it twisted, white boy. We ain't related. Not sort of or any otha'way. Feel me?"

"I was just a...."

G-Killa turned to the black/purple youth and said, "2-Black, go inside and get Lil' Smokey."

Without hesitating, 2-Black double stepped it back into the house.

"So, you're married to Winston's mother, Gloria, huh?"

G-Killa snorted, "Of course. What you think. We—"

"Daddy, does cousin Winston live here?" Headley asked as he and Fred were suddenly behind me.

"Dayuum!" G-Killa screeched. "What the Mutha—" He drew out his 40-caliber pistol from his waistband and pointed it at my two boys. His other two homies followed suit. I twirled around and set my body in front of my kids, my arms spread out wide. "Don't shoot!"

I shouted frantically. "They're my sons!"

From the front porch of the house, a woman's voice called out. "Gerald put down your gun!"

Gloria, Winston's mother, bolted from the porch and stood next to me in the line of fire. "Y'all put your guns down!"

In slow motion, G-Killa and his two homies set their weapons back in their waistbands.

"What's wrong wit yo kids?" questioned G-Killa, examining Fred and Headley.

Headley spoke before I could open my mouth. "Actually, there's nothing wrong with us.

My brother, Fred, just doesn't have a head. Technically, we're conjoined twins. Oh, shoot. Where're my manners. I'm Headley, and below me, is my older brother, Fred, by 5 minutes, give or take a few seconds."

G-Killa cringed.

"You one ugly little mo' fo'."

G-Killa's two homies agreed by laughing.

"Gerald!" Gloria's voice was harsh.

"Hey, that's not polite!" My voice was harsher. "My son's are beautiful. We have a first place baby-beauty pageant trophy to prove it, Mr G-Killa."

"You mean uh ugly-baby pageant trophy," taunted G-Killa, as his homies' laughter turned to wails.

Fred clenched his fists, and Headley curled his lip and shot G-Killa a laser-beam leer like he wanted to eat that big oaf's brain. I was sure my boys sensed that G-Killa was a criminal, but they needed more proof, for G-Killa and his homies could be gun-toting Republicans.

"You are so crude, Gerald," Gloria said to G-Killa. Then she turned to the boys and me. "Come on, Fred and Headley, let's go inside and meet your cousin Winston. I'm Winston's mother, Gloria."

"Hey, white boy, take off dat red cap and shirt befo' you step in da house. No Blood colours here, feel me?" G-Killa had a serious expression.

I didn't feel him at all, but I took heed, not wanting any more trouble. I excused myself to retrieve Mildead from the car and to put on a new shirt—a blue one. When Mildead and I soon entered the house, Gloria led my little family to Winston's bedroom, where my nephew was laid up in bed, recuperating from a gunshot wound to the shoulder.

The first thing I noticed about Winston was his large, reddish-brown afro, the '60s and 70's revisited. The second thing I noticed was his light-complexioned skin, nearly the colour of a worn-out page of book, and the tiny light-brown freckles that sprinkled his sharp nose and pancake cheeks. The kid was indeed a looker.

"So, you're my uncle Filmon," Winston said, propping himself up against the bed's headboard.

"I'd heard a lot about you from my pops. By telephone, anyway."

My nephew's comment cut at my heart. I knew my brother had rarely visited his son, but at least Zeke had sent regular child support payments.

"I think I was around fifteen when you were born," I said, shaking his hand. I then turned to the side and made introductions.

"This beautiful woman is Mildead, and these two little fellows are our sons and your cousins, Fred and Headley."

My boys moved hesitantly from behind Mildead in full view of Winston's raised eyebrows.

"Hello, cousin Winston. I'm Headley, and my lower half is my older brother Fred."

Winston went silent for a brief moment, eyeing his little cousins from head to toe and down again to toe. "Wassup, I'm Winston. My pops wrote me about you two. Come here, gimme some love, little cuzzes."

Winston threw out his good arm, offering the boys an embrace.

Fred and Headley wasted no time and hopped on the bed, giving their cousin big warm hugs.

Smiles were all around.

Winston set Fred and Headley on his lap. "You two are sho' unique. Not too many kids look like you. And that's a good thing. It wouldn't be an interestin' world if everybody looked alike, feel me?"

Headley smiled. "I feel you."

Fred followed with two thumbs up.

My heart warmed. That was the nicest comment anyone had said to my boys.

"Are you sick, cousin Winston?" Headley asked, genuinely concerned.

"Nah, some fools shot me," Winston replied, pushing out his bandaged shoulder.

Fred signed a quick remark.

"Yeah," agreed Headley. "Fred said, let's go kick their butts."

Winston laughed and put out his fist. "My niggas."

Fred and Headley immediately picked up on the gesture and bumped fists with their cousin.

"My nigga," returned Headley.

Everyone chuckled except for me. I didn't get the N-word connotation. I gotta keep up with social media or at least start texting, I thought.

I asked Winston if he knew who shot him.

"Yeah. Bloods."

"Bloods?"

"A rival gang of my step pop's gang, the Crips. I was walkin' to the crib, and I got caught in the crossfire between a Blood drive-by and my step pop and his homies returning fire."

"That's horrible," I said, shaking my head. "Are you a Crip?"

"Nah. It's not my thang."

"Oh, I didn't allow it," Gloria blurted out. "My husband Gerald had been a Crip for years. I didn't know he was in a gang until after we were married. And, he wanted my Winston to join. But unh unh, no way. Not my baby."

Winston lifted Fred and Headley an inch from his lap to adjust his posture, so to get more comfortable.

"But G-Killa' keeps pushing me to be in the gang; he thinks it'll make me a man. I'm just sixteen, and I nearly got myself killed by association. I wanna make it to seventeen."

Gloria covered her face with her hands and began to tear up. "Filmon, I don't know what I'm going to do. Winston's my only child. I worry every time he leaves the house."

I put my arm around Gloria's shoulder, consoling her. "Why don't you move...leave this place."

"We tried not too long ago. But my husband found us at my friend's house and forced us back here," said Gloria, wiping away tears.

"What about the police?"

Winston scoffed. "That's no good. G-Killa's an OG shot caller in the Crips. Even if he went to prison, he'd order other Crip members on the outside to get us."

"OG?"

"Original Gangsta."

That's original, I thought to myself. "So your stepfather G-Killa is a bad guy, huh."

Winston took a gander past me to see if anyone was outside his bedroom listening in. When he saw no one, he replied, "He's the worst kind. A drug dealer, a robber, and a real killer—just like his name. So are his homies, 2-Black, J-Rock, and Lenny."

I pulled my head back. "Lenny?"

"Oh, he's new...just started. He hadn't given himself a gang name yet."

"Oh, okay." I turned to Gloria and set my hands on her shoulders, looking deep into her eyes and said. "Don't worry. We'll figure something out." I then gave Milead and the boys that we-got-some-work-to-do look.

Mildead returned a knowing nod and a wink. Fred, a soft thumbs up, and then Headley squealed.

"Are we gonna eat their brains, daddy?"

I rolled my eyes back hard in my head and shot Headley a cringing eye and thought to myself, this boy got the biggest mouth this side of the Mississippi.

"What was that, Headley?" asked Gloria.

I beat my son's big mouth with my fast mouth.

"Oh, he said, are we going to...um... Easter Parade."

"No, I didn't, daddy."

I slapped Headley with my eyes. "Yes, you did, son."

Fred poked Headley in the stomach.

"Ouch.... Oh, yeah. I...I did say that, sorry."

"But Easter's six months from now, Headley," Gloria pointed out.

Headley glanced at my searing eyes before he replied to Gloria. "Uh...I guess I just wanted to get a head start."

Gloria bent over Winston's bed and lightly pinched Headley's cheek. "You are so cute."

We spent the rest of the afternoon trading family stories until Gloria invited us to stay the night. I declined respectfully, for my little family needed to spend some quality time with G-Killa and his homies. From the front porch, Gloria and Winston waved their goodbyes, as we were making our way back to the car. And sitting in a black Range Rover, which was parked behind our Pacer, were G-Killa and the rest of the Crips smoking a fat marijuana joint. Before my little family stepped into our car, I whispered to them an impromptu plan.

"Got it?" I said, as soon as I finished telling them the plan.

Mildead and the boys nodded excitedly.

I spun away from Mildead and the boys and walked over to the Range Rover, sticking my nose inches away from its closed driver-side window. The window soon rolled down smoothly, letting out a cloud of marijuana smoke that smothered my face. I coughed like I had cancer of the lung.

"What's the matter, white boy, can't hang?" teased G-Killa, materialising as the smoke was clearing.

"I'm not much into marijuana. I prefer the heavier drugs," I admitted, wiping away the remnants of the smoke from my face.

"Whoa!" G-Killa ejected. He then turned to his homies and said, "Dis fool inta heavya drugs."

All four Crips laughed in harmony.

"What kinda drugs ya inta, Blood?" asked 2-Black from the passenger seat, mocking me for wearing the Blood gang colours earlier in the day.

I made a show of looking behind me and at both flanks, checking if anyone was within earshot.

"That's why I came up to you gentlemen. I want to buy some cracker. A whole lot of cracker."

G-Killa eyed me like I was crazy. "Cracker? Ya mean...crack?"

"Oh, yeah. Crack."

More laughter from inside the Ranger Rover.

"So ya wanna buy some crack, white boy? I gotta few rocks on hand." G-Killa winked.

"Rocks?"

"Pieces. Small pieces of crack—dey look like rocks."

"Oh, I see. No. I want to buy a boulder of crack, please," I said with a straight face.

G-Killa looked to his homies again. "Dis cracka sump'em else." He gave his attention back to me and said, "Ya mean a kilo?"

"Oh, yeah. A kilo. My girlfriend and I have a suitcase full of money for a kilo of cracker...I mean crack." Even though G-Killa was a criminal, I felt a tinge of guilt for lying.

G-Killa snatched the back of my head with his massive hand and pulled my whole upper body in the Range Rover, my legs dangling in the air. Before I took my next breath, his 40-caliber pistol was pressed up against my forehead.

"Ya betta not be Po Po, fool. Are ya Po Po?" G-Killa's tone was ominous.

I was shivering from fright. "Wha.... What? Po Po?"

"Po Po. Police, nigga."

Although I was scared to death, I was also pleased he finally saw through the colour of my pale skin. It was time to present the race card.

"It's quite ironic that you'd called me the N-word, Mr G-Killa. I have African American blood in me since my ancestor was a black slave. So, we may actually be related."

G-Killa shook his head in disbelief and glanced back at his homies. "Dis fool's no Po Po. I bet ma life on dat, fo sho'."

"Bet ma life, too," agreed 2-Black.

Two more similar wagers from the backseat.

G-Killa took his gun away from my forehead and said, "I don't have dat much merchandise here.

But I can go get it. Ya have at least $25,000 in yo suitcase?"

"Yep."

"Gimme da money. Den I'll go get da kilo."

I wiggled my body back out of the Range Rover. "Mr G-Killa, I wasn't born yesterday morning, you know. Me and my family would have to go with you to get that kilo. That's not-negotiable."

"All 'ight. Y'all wanna squeeze in here or follow us in ya funky-ass car?"

I presented a sly, wide grin. "My family will squeeze in with you gentlemen."

Gloria awoke at 6:15 am as usual to fetch the morning paper. She opened the front door, hoping the paperboy hadn't missed the front porch this time. She smiled when the newspaper was at her feet, next to an envelope with her name on it. Dismissing the newspaper, Gloria picked up the envelope, opened it, and she began to read:

Dear Gloria,

I am leaving you forever. And I am taking my homies 2-Black, J-Rock, and yes, even Lenny, along with me. But I am leaving you the Range Rover—there's no need for it where we're going. Also, in the glove department is a wad of cash, which was earned from selling cracker ... I mean crack. And don't bother calling the potpourri, for I am NOT a missing person. I am going back to the Motherland, the deepest part of Africa, where no living or dead human being, will ever be found. So I will NEVER ever come back. Good bye.

Love,
Mr G-Killa
P.S. Tell Filmon, he was a nice and handsome guy.

Gloria didn't know what to think of what she had just read, but she knew for a fact that the letter hadn't been written by Gerald aka G-Killa. She took out the Range Rover key from the envelope, holding it firmly in her hand. Then she smiled as she remembered what Filmon had said to her: Don't worry. We'll figure something out.

CHAPTER 12

Hurray for Hollywood!

GETTING RID OF G-KILLA and his Crips hadn't been easy. Nevertheless, my little family got the job done. I needed a doughnut. So before we would cruise Hollywood boulevard to movie star watch, we stopped at a doughnut shop across from the Wiltern Theatre, on the corner of Wilshire and Western, in Korea town. Typically, a venue for live music, the Wiltern had a special offering of horror films since it was Halloween night. As soon as I chomped down on my doughnut, as my family of human flesh eaters watched, we decided to delay the cruising and go across the street to see Zombie Zumba, a film about out-of-shape zombies toning up before brain-eating. After the film, as we were heading toward our car, an inspired Fred signed, asking me to enroll him in Zumba classes. Although Headley had other aspirations, the acting bug had bit him hard.

"Daddy, I wanna be in the movies."

"What? You don't want to be a Wildlife Waste Hand."

"Hey, great costume, kid!" a costumed Dracula said, as he passed us by.

Headley pointed at himself, and Fred did the same thing. "Who me?"

The Dracula turned around and began to slowly walk backward. "Yeah. I like your costume."

"But I'm not wearing a costume," Headley said.

"Oh, I'm sor.... Ew, gross."

Headley felt hurt and angry at the same time. "Keep walking, you butthole vampire, before I drink your blood. And I'm not kidding."

The costumed Dracula felt Headley's serious vibes, then he made an in-motion about face and high-stepped it off.

"Daddy, let's go eat his brain," fumed Headley.

I knelt down, holding Fred's shoulders and kissed Headley's forehead. "Son, I don't think he's a bad person. He's just ignorant and doesn't understand the true meaning of beauty in someone. And, you can't go around eating people just because they hurt your feelings. Understand?"

"I understand, daddy," replied Headley. "But what if he had hurt your feelings?"

"Then you could eat his fake Dracula butt.... Just kidding," I smiled.

"You're funny, daddy. I love you."

"Aw...I love you, too, son." I quickly gave my attention to Fred before he felt I was leaving him out. "And yes, I love you, Fred."

Fred reached up and hugged me around my neck.

I suddenly remembered Headley's comment about wanting to be in the movies.

"So Headley, you changed your mind about wanting to be a Wildlife Waste Handler?"

"No, daddy. Not at all. I'm still too young to be a Wildlife Waste Handler, but I'm not too young to be in the movies."

"Good point, son," I knelt back down and rubbed Fred's chest. "And what about you, Fred? You wanna be in the movies, too? You could still take Zumba classes."

Fred tilted his posture and folded his arms, contemplating. A minute passed by.

"Fred, did you hear me?" I was getting impatient.

"He's still thinking, daddy," said Headley, who seemed to have more patience than his father. After another minute passed by and a couple of impatient sighs from me, Fred finally signed his answer. It was a go.

"All right, good. Let's see about getting you two in the movies. Or, at least commercials."

Headley frowned and shook his head. "No commercials, daddy. I refuse to be a slave to the advertising process that perpetuate the widespread brainwashing of the masses."

"You'll get paid and might get free stuff."

"Oh, cool. Never mind then, I'll do commercials."

One of my jobs as a father was to help my sons realize their dreams and aspirations. My dream had been to become a Wildlife Waste Handler. With hard work and determination, I had made that dream come true. My first day on the job had been the happiest day of my life, next to the birth of my sons. I wanted Fred and Headley to have that same wonderful feeling I had. My sons wanted to be in the movies, and since we were in Los Angeles, the movie capital in the world, we might as well go for it. Of course, our objective of ridding the world of wickedness was still in play. But evil was everywhere. Even in Hollywood land.

I didn't know one thing about getting into the movies. But before we did anything, we needed a home base to get situated. I thought about asking Gloria and Winston to put us up at their place, but I didn't want us to be around there if the potpourri were to start asking questions of G-Killa's whereabouts. Headley might give us away with that big mouth of his, I mused to myself. We eventually found a motel in the heart of Hollywood land, near Hollywood and Vine—arguably, second to Haight/Ashbury of San Francisco, as the most famous cross streets in the world.

I went online and learned that the boys needed to get headshots and an agent. Also, a bio, if the boys had any acting experience. Online acting experts, Katie from Minnesota and Josh from Iowa, had suggested that Fred and Headley audition for theatrical plays to get their feet wet in the business. When I'd brought that up to the boys, they instantly shot it down. Headley had figured that acting in theatre would only slow up their journey on the road to fame. Fred had agreed. I then looked up the many talent agencies that was listed in the Los Angeles area. I found a perfect one: Mort's Talent Agency for Children.

Getting headshots wasn't as easy as I'd thought it would be. One photographer, after seeing Fred and Headley, had fainted, hitting his head on the corner of a desk, dying instantly. Although we had been shocked and saddened by that unfortunate circumstance, it was also an ideal opportunity for Mildead and the boys to have lunch without any strenuous effort. Another photographer had put up a closed sign as soon as he'd seen us walking toward his shop. Finally, we'd found a photographer, but he did have his troubles getting the right angles to shoot his pics. To get an upright photo of Headley's face, Headley had to struggle to stand on his feet while Fred dangled in the air. Both had a difficult time, yet they endured. I was so proud.

For Fred and Headley's bio, I listed all of the boys' talents and attributes, such as Headley's singing and overall genius, and Fred's amazing agility, hoping that whoever would read it would forgive my sons' inexperience in acting. Though, for the pièce de résistance, I listed their first-place victory in the 11th Annual Herman's Donuts' Baby Pageant. I was pretty sure that would get any agent excited to get my boys in his or her camp. So with the headshots and bio in hand, we were off to see Mort.

Mort's Talent Agency was located in a depleted neighbourhood within the city of Inglewood, another one of those subsidiary municipalities pockmarking the greater Los Angeles area. We found excellent parking in a pretty-blue parking space, right out front of the talent agency's office, which was squeezed between Saul's Taco Diner and Maury's Kosher Soul Food Restaurant. Evidently, the beginnings of a gentrified block.

"All right, boys. Put your game faces on," I said, "we're gonna approach this audition just like the baby pageant. And Headley, if you're asked to sing, what song are you gonna do?"

Headley put on a sly, little smile. "Can I rap Yo Momma Got Booty this time?"

I hit the boy with an exasperated glare.

"Just kidding, daddy. I'll stick with Truly Scrumptious."

Fred signed something that I didn't catch.

"What was that, Fred?"

Fred slowed his signing.

"No. You can't break dance while Headley sings Truly Scrumptious. It's not compatible. Just stick with the subtle ballet moves you two had worked out. And don't give me the Finger." The boy was itchin' to give to me, I thought to myself.

A small bell jingled when I opened the agency's office door. A voluptuous blonde secretary with a tight, knee-hi skirt and a well fitting, really well fitting, pink cashmere sweater, greeted Mildead and I, with a charming smile. Until, her eyes came down upon Fred and Headley—then her smile converted into a gape. She recovered nicely and returned in character.

"Hello. May I help you?" the secretary said, trying hard not to stare at my boys.

I cleared my throat before I answered. "Yes. My two sons here, need an agent, so they can act in films." She gave up and let loose a long gander at Fred and Headley before she asked. "Um...do you have an appointment?"

"No, we don't. I thought my boys could just audition for Mort."

"That's not how it works. First, you have to leave your son's headshots and bios with us. Then, if Mr Lipshitz likes what he sees, he'll call you to audition your sons."

"Mr Lipschitz?"

The secretary lowered her voice. "That's Mort. Mort Lipshitz."

I saw Headley cover his mouth, so not to crack up. But Fred bent over, holding his tummy, laughing in silence.

"Miss, we came along way. Is there any way we can see Mr Lipshitz today. My sons are very talented."

"I'm sorry. Mr Lipshitz is very busy. He—"

"Pardon me, Miss," interrupted Headley. He then turned on the dramatics. "My brother and I have a dream. A dream to be thespians of the big screen...just until we're old enough to follow in our dear father's footsteps as Wildlife Waste Handlers. But we believe our time is now to be actors, for the world awaits us."

The secretary was in awe of Headley's diction. "How old are you?"

"We're one and a half, going on three-quarters next month."

"No way. You can't be only one and a half. You—"

"They're big for their age. And, baby geniuses," I said proudly, cutting her off.

The secretary gave the boys another good once-over before she said, "Just to be sure. You are two different individuals, right?"

"Right. I'm Headley, and the tall one below is my conjoined twin, Fred. He doesn't have a head."

Fred waved his greeting.

"I have to show both of you to Mr Lipshitz. Have a seat. I'll just be a moment."

The secretary hurried back to her desk and made a phone call. She whispered a few words in the receiver, hung up, and walked over to a door at the rear of the office, slipping into another room.

"Hey, daddy," Headley said, tugging on my pants pocket.

"Yes, son?"

"The Mort your Lip-Shitz. The more your butt talks. Ha! Ha!"

I had to crack up on that one.

The secretary soon returned and smiled, "Mr Lipshitz will see you now."

Mort Lipshitz's office was cluttered with stacks of books on a carpeted floor, near a large oak desk, which was also burdened with bios and headshots that was piled up so high, Mr Lipshitz himself could hardly be seen sitting on his chair, doodling on a sheet of paper. The walls were lined with photos of famous child actors and the not-so-famous—all Mr Lipshitz's clients at one time or another.

Without raising his head, Mr Lipshitz set his hand, palm up, on a stack of headshots, and he then wiggled his fingers. "Okay. Let's see the kids' headshots."

"Cert...certainly, Mr Lipshitz. Here you go," I said with a nervous tone, then I handed him the pics.

Mr Lipshitz hand came right back up with what I had given him. "These aren't headshots. It's a menu for Saul's Taco Diner."

"Oh, sorry." I snatched the menu out of his hand and went on a frantic eye search for the headshots.

"Here, daddy," said Headley, raising the pics.

Within a second, Mr Lipshitz had the headshots in his hand. Within two seconds, he popped his head over the pile of bios and headshots, and he shot to his feet. His widened eyes stretched his wrinkly face as they set upon my two boys. The man looked like he was a hundred years old, but I could tell he still had some feistiness in him by the way he moved like a much younger man.

"Miss Epstein said there were two fascinating, unusual boys outside my office," said Mr Lipshitz. "I see unusual. Now, show me fascinating."

Fred and Headley waved a greeting. "How do you do, Mr Lipschitz. My name is Headley Trout, and this is my brother, Fred Trout, holding me up. We would like to

perform a song and dance number for your viewing."
Headley then looked down at his brother. "Hit it, Fred."

Fred snapped his fingers and did a graceful pirouette
before Headley went into the song.

My eyes kept roaming back and forth from my boys
and Mr Lipschitz. I couldn't pick up any vibes at all from
the old man—he was stone-faced. That worried me a little. Yet I had all the confidence in the world in my
talented sons. My sight veered off and caught Mildead
transfixed over our children just being themselves. She
had been quiet all this time, though the pride in her eyes
sang its own song, loud and vivid enough for me to grasp
in my heart.

Headley was at the tail end of Truly Scrumptious,
"...My heart beats so unruly, and I also love you, honest
truly, I do."

Fred then bent over in a Shakespearean bow.

The stoned face of Mr Lipshitz was no more—a grin
bloomed through its hard exterior. "That was wonderful,
boys!" praised Mr Lipshitz. "Not since the great Shirley
Temple, has there been a child act such as yours."

"Shirley Temple?" said Headley.

"She was a triple threat, my boy. A singer, dancer, and
a wonderful actress. The greatest child star of our time."

"Cool," Headley exhaled. "Did she rap, too?"

Mr Lipshitz put on a bewildered face.

"Rap?"

"Yeah. You know, like this.... Yo momma got booty and yo daddy all moody, 'cause he foolin'wit a ho who stankin' wit cooties. All the—"

I muffled my boy's mouth with my hand before he might've spat off some F-words or grabbed his own crotch.

The old man smiled.

"No. I don't think she rapped, son. But I'm sure if Shirley had wanted to, she could've done so."

"Cool."

Mr Lipshitz glanced at Fred and Headley's bio and said to me, "I see the boys don't have acting experience, and I—"

"Oh, they can act," I blurted, "They're natural born actors."

"Can they read yet?"

"Headley can read, speak, and write in seven different languages. And Fred reads braille, a master in sign language, and he's currently working on Native American smoke signals."

Mr Lipshitz nodded, impressed.

He reached over to one of the stacks on his desk and grabbed a movie script, offering it to Headley.

"Here you go. You're Headley, right?"

"Yes," Headley said. "What is this?"

"It's a movie script. Sides in Hollywood lingo. Read the part of Billy, right here in the first

scene." Mr Lipshitz pointed to the lower part of the script's second page.

"Okay."

"And I'll read the part of Billy's friend, Sally. Now in this scene, their friend Tom, had gone missing... All right, I'll start it off... Billy, I...I don't know where Tom could be."

Headley took a deep breath before transforming himself into the Billy character. "I'm sure he was kidnapped by that gang of zombie midgets, Sally." Headley then raised a fist. "But with God as my witness, I shall hunt down those little brain-eaters, using this golden slingshot! And I will return Tom to us! Hopefully, in one piece. Then, we will once again be the three amigos. Forever and ever... And ever!"

With teary eyes, Mr Lipshitz blew his nose with his handkerchief, and then sniffled, "That was so beautiful, Headley. So realistic. I'd be honoured to have you and your brother as my clients."

"Cool!"

My boys' new agent, Mortimer Lipshitz, went to work right away, and within a week he procured Fred and

Headley's first gig. A Head & Shoulders dandruff shampoo commercial for children. The commercial opened up with the boys in a shower...without showing their little winkies, of course, washing Headley's hair with the Head & shoulders' shampoo. Headley's only line was, "My brother and I don't need two heads to use Head & Shoulders shampoo." Then Fred gave two thumbs up. After the first and only take, everyone on the set, including the Head & Shoulders' execs, congratulated the boys, believing a hit commercial was in the works.

My little family and I were ecstatic. We got in the car and sped off to Mr Lipshitz's office. We soon told the old man what everyone on the set had said, but Mr Lipshitz did his best to bring us down from the clouds.

"Mr Trout, even if the commercial is a national hit, it doesn't mean that film roles are just going to fall in the boys' laps. Hollywood is a tough, unforgiving business." Mr Lipshitz had a no-nonsense tone.

I retaliated. "Well, Hollywood hasn't seen anything like my boys before."

"No one has seen anything like your boys before."

I patted the old man's back. "That's my point, Mr Lipshitz. Just tell Cecil B. DeMille we're on our way!"

"Mr Demille's been dead for decades."

"Well, tell Alfred Hitchcock then, baby!"

• CHAPTER 13 •

(Los Angeles, Meet Two More Zombies and One Serial Killer)

Hollywood boulevard flowed east to west, cutting through acres of land in the city of Los Angeles. Every day thousands of vehicles cruised along this world-famous thoroughfare, carrying all kinds of people from all sorts of places. But on this particular day, Hollywood boulevard was host to a dark blue van that carried two zombies and a serial killer who wasn't there to see any famous landmarks.

"All right, how do we find this sister of yours among these millions of people?" asked James, feeling tired from the long drive.

"My sister's boyfriend has a relative in Compton. We should drive there and pick up a phone book or something, and check if there's a Trout listed," replied Toodead, and at the same time drooling over the many pedestrians on the street.

"So, Trout is the surname of the boyfriend?"

"Yes. His name is Filmon Trout."

James stared blankly as he pulled up the van at a red light. "That name sounds familiar. Hmm ...

I can't think of where I'd heard that name of Trout before. It...it'll come to me."

"I'm hungry," Sodead whined.

"You just ate the last remains of that dead girl, an hour ago," said James.

Toodead defended her sister. "We're zombies, J.T. We're always hungry."

"All right, we'll make a stop."

Sodead smiled wickedly and rubbed her hands together. "Goody."

James raised an index finger. "But, we need to wait another hour or so when it gets dark."

Sodead pouted like a little girl, not getting what she wanted. "Shit balls."

Los Angeles was a serial killer's paradise. The city was full of runaways, drug addicts, and out-of-work actors, all of whom society had forgotten. Whereas to the zombie sisters, Los Angeles was just another city. Their means of sustenance walked about in every city, town or hamlet in the country.

The night came fast, and the three killers grew anxious.

"What about that guy?" Sodead blurted out, pointing to a large man standing at a bus stop.

James squashed Sodead's suggestion. "Too big. And, he looks Samoan. It would be too much work for me." He failed to mention that the only men he killed were reality TV stars and gay astronauts from the ghetto who were hard to find.

"You're big," Sodead popped off.

"That's true. But in my field, it's always better to prey on the ones who seem weaker than you.

"Not big-ass Samoans."

Both Sodead and Toodead instantly had the same thought—also, big women who knew karate.

James whistled a long, drawn-out note. "There's a little chocolate honey I can easily handle."

A petite African American woman was standing on the corner, enticing passersby with her suggestive air grinding of the hips. She wore a shiny, red short-cropped wig that topped her head and a scant gold-coloured bikini-like outfit, which could also be used as eye patches, barely covering her female valuables.

"Yeah. She's okay by me," smiled Sodead.

"Me, too," agreed Toodead.

"Well, then, let's say hi," smirked James.

James Thomas Fenimore eased the van to a complete stop, right in front of the prostitute who smiled and made a hand gesture, to roll down the passenger window.

Sodead complied.

"Hey, ya'll. Wassup," greeted the woman, showing a gold upper-front tooth.

"What's up with you, girl," returned James.

The woman squinted in the van. "How many uh ya in there?"

"Oh, it's just these two ladies and me. You need a lift?"

The woman was always suspicious of vans. "Uh...I don't know. Look like too many uh ya white folks for me."

James took out two one-hundred-dollar bills and flashed it in front of him. "I got some money to spend."

The sight of large bills piqued the woman's interest. "How much ya wanna spend?"

"Two hundred dollars for everything."

"Three hundred dollars. 'Cause there three uh ya."

James smiled. "Deal. Hop on in."

Seconds after the woman had entered the van, her muffled scream vibrated against James' palm.

Subduing the prostitute had been more difficult than James had thought it would be—she was like a caged animal clawing to survive, yet the serial killer liked it that way. The more the women fought, the more he became aroused. Petite women were his usual targets. Larger women usually put up more of a fight, which he liked, but they also had a better chance to escape. James could have allowed Sodead and Toodead to join in on the kill, but he wanted the sisters to see how he operated. And, to let them know what could happen to them if they decided to turn on him.

James chopped the prostitute's body into small pieces—snacks for Sodead and Toodead. At the back of his van was a four-by-four-foot freezer, bolted to the floor and plugged into a small generator.

A large cutting board was glued atop the freezer door, facilitating his expertise in the use of cutlery.

"Let's get a motel room. I'm exhausted. We'll head out to Compton in the morning," said James.

Both sisters agreed.

At a decrepit Hollywood motel, James set up the sisters with their room. Even though he felt an inherent kinship with Sodead and Toodead, there was no way he was going to sleep in the same room with them. *I'm sure they feel the same way*, James thought. James was so tired when he entered his room, and he knocked out as soon as he closed his eyes. As flashes of the prostitute highlighted his dream, heavy thuds on his motel room door mercilessly forced him awake. When he reluctantly opened the door, Sodead and Toodead ran into his room and turned on the television to channel 2.

"That's Fred and Headley on TV!" shouted Toodead.

Fred and Headley's Head & Shoulders' commercial just tuned out. James caught the last word of Headley's pitch.

"Who's Fred and Headley?"

"They're our sister Mildead's two boys."

"Those...whatever-they-were...boys in the shower?"

Toodead nodded hard. "Yes."

James sat in silence while his mind worked out details. And then he said, "A Head and Shoulders' commercial, huh? Maybe we don't have to go to Compton after all."

James woke up the next morning, feeling confident that he may be able to find Mildead for the twin sisters. At 9 am sharp, he went online, using his smartphone and perused the relevant websites regarding the recent Head & Shoulders' commercial. Then he made four phone calls. The last call was to Mort's Talent Agency.

Toodead and Sodead felt their sister Mildead's presence, but they weren't sure how close she was. The twin sisters sat in James' van, as it moved steadily along Hollywood boulevard. They eyed every parked car, every car that passed, and every human being in between their peripheral vision. Filmon's orange 1978 Pacer wasn't too difficult to spot. Neither was Fred and Headley. They frowned at each failed attempt to catch sight of their sister, yet at least they had a solid lead. Thanks to the efforts of their new serial killer friend.

Miss Epstein looked up from her desk and smiled at the large man and two attractive but odd-looking women who just entered the office. She instantly assessed the ladies' poor taste in makeup and clothing. *Who wears green makeup and a nurse's outfit in public,* she thought.

"Good day. How may I help you?"

James smiled and answered, "We're looking for the mother of clients of yours. The clients are two little boys, Fred and Headley." He then motioned toward the twin sisters. "These two ladies are the boys' aunts and the sisters of the boys' mother, Mildead."

Miss Epstein showed disappointing eyes. "I'm so sorry. I can't give out any personal information regarding the boys and their parents. But I can leave a message for them."

James examined Miss Epstein's entire body, restraining himself from what he did best—kill. He despised the way her red hair settled atop her bare shoulders and the way she wore her tight blouse, pressing against her breasts. *I know she's a loose woman*, his mind whispered.

"Excuse me, sir?" Miss Epstein said, trying to get James' attention subtly. "Sir, do you want to leave a message for the boys' mother? Sir?"

James broke out of his reverie. "Oh, pardon me. Can I speak to your boss?"

"He's out for the day."

"So is there anyone else who I can talk to?"

"No, sir. I'm the only one here."

James turned to Sodead and Toodead and whispered, "Are you girls hungry?"

Sodead's eyes popped wide open. "We're always hungry."

James smirked and said, "All right then, girls. It's your turn."

Sodead leered at the secretary. "Brain..."

James entered Mr Lipshitz's private office while Sodead and Toodead feasted on Miss Epstein's bloodied brain. He looked around the cluttered room to see if there was a filing cabinet. There were only three black-leather chairs and dozens of folders stacked on the floor and atop a brown double pedestal desk.

"Why doesn't this guy get a couple of filing cabinets like everybody else," James muttered to himself, regretting entering the office.

He walked up to the desk, and an immediate smile came upon his face. A folder with Fred and Headley's name on it was conspicuously displayed—the only folder laid out on the desk, not on a pile.

James picked up the folder and opened it. Another smile appeared on his face when the boys' Los Angeles address protruded from their bio page. "Easy peasy."

James and the zombie sisters left Mort's Talent Agency in bloody disarray. They got into the van and drove off toward Hollywood boulevard and Vine street. It was a straightforward drive back from Inglewood to Hollywood. They stayed on La Brea Boulevard and took it all the way until they hit Hollywood boulevard in 25 minutes.

"Easy peasy," James muttered softly. When he turned left on Hollywood boulevard, he glanced at the address on the bio page.

"You know what," James said, "I think our motel is close to this address where your sister is at...Wait, we're almost there."

James bent over the steering wheel, looking out at the different buildings and addresses. Next to a parking lot was the Motel Josette—their destination.

"Do you believe this...our motel is around the freakin' corner."

Sodead and Toodead gazed at each other and grinned. For they knew their zombie intuition that had sensed Mildead was near, had been spot on.

"J.T., we need to separate Filmon from my sister and the boys," Toodead said. "If Filmon is out of the way, I believe my sister Mildead, along with the boys, will return to Sodead and me."

"And then we will be one happy family again," Sodead joined in.

"Why don't we just do away with Filmon as soon as we see him, whether or not Mildead and the boys are there?" James said impatiently.

Toodead eyed James as though he had asked a stupid question. "Because Mildead and the boys will fight to the death for him."

"But Mildead is just one woman, and the boys are little kids. We could handle them."

Sodead barged into the conversation, "Ha! Mildead is like the alpha zombie among us sisters.

"And those two little boys—they're vicious monsters when they want to be. Especially if you mess with their father."

"Wait. Hold up. You mean to tell me that your sister is also a zombie?"

"Yes," confirmed Toodead, "and Fred and Headley are half zombies, but they still eat human flesh."

James had an incredulous expression.

"All right. I thought I, a serial killer, and you two, zombies, were a crazy outfit.... Okay, here's what we're going to do..."

Sodead and Toodead huddled together and listened carefully.

"I'll go up alone to their motel room and ask for Filmon while you both wait here in the van. On my way there, I'll figure out a way to get the dude outta of the room. Then, I'll bring him back here to the van, where you two will be waiting to eat his brain. Good plan?"

"Good plan." the sisters replied simultaneously.

James left Sodead and Toodead, licking their lips on the prospect of eating Filmon's brain. Of all the humans in the world, the sisters desired the little brain of that nuisance of a man the most. Their excitement turned sour when James came back just a short while and by himself.

"There's no one home," said James as soon as he opened the driver-side door.

Sodead slapped her own knee in frustration. "Shit balls."

James turned on the radio to a Classic Rock station. "We'll wait awhile. If they don't show up soon, I'll call the number that was listed next to their address."

"Why don't you call now?" blurted Toodead.

"I'm tired. Just keep a lookout while I take a nap. And you better not eat me."

"Then don't sleep too long, big boy," Sodead said good-humoredly.

James wasn't sure if Sodead's remark was in jest. He promptly brought up his 12-inch hunting knife and held it under his windbreaker jacket...just in case.

CHAPTER 14

(Fred and Headley, Hollywood's Newest Stars)

My little family and I were sitting with the boys' agent Mort Lipshitz, inside Maury's Kosher Soul Food restaurant, celebrating Fred and Headley's signing of their co-starring roles in the Independent Studios/Bollywood production of Mahatma Zombie, starring teenage Pop singing sensation, Dustin Beaver.

"Eat up, Mildead. You, too, boys. There's plenty of bagels with barbecued lox. Oh, yeah, this place uses the same barbecue sauce as the previous owner, Tyrone, who also sold Maury the ingredients," said Mr Lipshitz.

"Um...Mr Lipshitz. Mildead and the boys are on a special diet. They've already eaten. But I'll eat anything."

I was quite pleased that I hadn't lied. My family were in fact on a special diet, and they had just eaten a young man who'd tried to snatch an old lady's purse. I had been duly impressed with Fred's running speed. He had caught the dude in three seconds flat. *Maybe after this movie business, I could enter my boys in junior track meets,* I thought.

"Oh, that's fine," said Mr Lipshitz. He then gave his attention to Fred and Headley.

"Alright, boys. Remember what the production assistant had said. You two are to report at Independent Studios in a couple of hours for a greet and meet session with the director and the other actors. So after we're done here head on down there, it only takes thirty minutes from here."

Mort gave me a side glance and said, "Mr Trout, make sure your sons get there on time to make a good first impression."

"Yes, I'll certainly do that. By the way, you can call me, Filmon."

"All right, Filmon. I will."

I showed a happy smile. "I'll call you Mort."

"Just stick with Mr Lipshitz."

"Oh...oh, okay. Old fart."

Independent Studios wasn't half the size of the major studios, but its last two pictures The Night of the Living Head and Zombie Hookers were international hits. Studio executives had figured that they would keep the momentum rolling by putting out a third straight horror flick. And with pop star Dustin Beaver signed on as the lead, Mahatma Zombie, would most likely be a surefire hit. If it weren't for the back to back motion picture hits, Independent Studios would have folded in bankruptcy, never to recover.

The head of the studio was Abasi Uba, the former president of the small West African country, Sierra Leone. Uba had been uprooted for embezzlement, by an army coup, and then he fearfully fled the country. The U.S. immediately gave him sanctuary in exchange for information on his secretive dealings with the Chinese government. He had later changed his name to Matumbe Dakimbo. With the embezzled money, the newly named Matumbe Dakimbo was able to purchase Independent Studios, formerly owned by a CIA exec, for the bargain price of twenty million dollars.

Twenty minutes before our meet and greet meeting was to start, I drove my family up to the studio lot gate and showed the security guard our pass. After giving

Fred and Headley a long gaze, the guard waved us in and pointed in the direction of a fuchsia-coloured building that looked like a miniature aeroplane hangar. The boys and I were stoked. We couldn't believe we were in an actual Hollywood studio, though Mildead didn't seem like she cared by her emotionless expression. I just took it as her being indifferent to human pleasures due to her being a full-fledged zombie. Thank goodness, my boys still enjoyed different things other than human brains.

As soon as we got out of the car, we negotiated a winding staircase that fronted the building and found ourselves in front of an armed security guard posting outside of double doors. Over the doors was a gold-plated sign that read MD Headquarters. When I saw the guard and the sign, my first thought was military complex. I later found out that MD stood for Matumbe Dakimbo, who we were about to meet.

Outside his office, Mr Dakimbo welcomed us with opened arms. He towered over us with his six-foot-six burly frame, and his skin was African dark—even darker than 2-Black's. His polite smile and country mannerisms put us at ease from the start. But what caught my attention was the six-inch scar that ran down his right cheek, which gave him a menacing appearance. He wore one of those white pastels coloured Guaybera shirts, the type Fidel Castro would wear, and on his feet were Birkenstock

Riva brown-leather sandals. Not the attire that I expected from a studio head. His English was perfect, but it had a smooth throaty accent associated with the African people, in which I found quite endearing.

"Ah...little Fred and Headley. Future movie stars. When I saw your commercial, I knew I had to have both of you in my new film," said Mr Dakimbo, as he bent over with his hands over his knees.

"Thank you for having us, sir," Headley replied. "We hope to compliment your film with our uniqueness."

Mr Dakimbo blew out a hearty laugh then said, "Yes. You two are certainly unique." He straightened up and brought his smile to Mildead and me.

"Mr and Mrs Trout, you must be very proud of your children."

I sputtered, for I wasn't sure if Mildead would bring up her no-ring-on-my-finger reply.

"Oh, yes. We are very proud."

Mildead just smiled and nodded.

"Come. Let us meet the other actors," Mr Dakimbo said.

The head of Independent Studios led us through a glass door that was next to his office.

Inside was a 400 x 300 square-foot room presenting a twelve-foot oval Hawaiian Koa conference table. And sitting on black Leya armchairs were the film's leading actress, and next to her was the director who was also a supporting actor, but there was no Dustin Beaver. Mr Dakimbo showed Mildead and the boys and I to our seats at the table, and he introduced us to the others as soon as we sat down.

Both actors popped their eyes out before offering their greetings to Fred and Headley. Maryan Kimble, a nine-teen-year-old first-time actress—your typical California blond—pretty, tanned and sexy, didn't hide her shocked expression, as did her co-actor Carter Grant, a not-so-typical chubby, brown-skinned actor/director from Hopatcong, New Jersey, whose real name was Mara Nete Bolobolo, who had entered the country illegally after he had snuck onto a cargo ship from Fiji.

"Mr Dakimbo, Dustin Beaver's not here yet?" said Headley, eyeing the entire room.

The studio head frowned. "He's running late...must be caught in traffic."

The door suddenly banged opened.

"Yo! Dustin's here, y'all! Please, don't get up!" shouted Dustin Beaver, with his arms spread out.

Dustin Sebastion Beaver, a thin-as-a-pole sixteen-year-old—the son of middle-class white parents from suburbia, skyrocketed to fame when he'd won a national singing competition at the age of fourteen. Although his music caters to mostly white teenaged girls, Dustin's lifestyle was akin to a gangsta rapper from the ghetto. Recently, he had been jailed two weeks for shooting a spitball at the mayor of Beverly Hills.

Everyone clapped at Dustin Beaver's dramatic entrance except me. I was the only one oblivious of the teenager's fame. Even Mildead clapped. I guess Dustin's fame also reached the zombie circles, I thought, impressed.

Fred and Headley obviously knew the teen sensation when they trotted his way. "Hi, Dustin! I'm Head—"

"Whoa! Get back, demon! Don't come a rushin' at me like that!" Dustin Beaver cried out, jumping back two feet. "What the hell are you?"

Headley was surprised by the pop star's reaction. "I...I'm..."

Mr Dakimbo interceded, "Dustin, these two boys are acting in the film with you. They play Pakistani zombie spies, posing as Indian zombies who are loyal to your character Mahatma zombie."

"Damn, they look like real freakin' zombies," said Dustin.

"Thank you," said Headley and Mildead, while Fred gave a thumbs up.

"I was sarcastic, you little freak."

"Hey, young man," I shouted at the teen brat, "name-calling is uncalled for!"

Dustin sneered at me then turned to Mr Dakimbo. "Who's this four-eyed fool?"

"This is Filmon Trout, the father of these boys," answered Mr Dakimbo.

Dustin feigned an apologetic expression. "Oh, I'm sorry...Not!"

"You're not cool at all," said Headley to Dustin.

Dustin mocked Headley, repeating what my son had said.

I'd had enough.

"Mr Dakimbo, I won't have my sons enduring this type of behaviour from that young man. I was hoping this would be an enjoyable experience for my boys. It hasn't been. Either Dustin Beaver goes, or my sons go."

Dustin laughed in our faces.

"Mr Trout, Dustin is the star of the picture," said Mr Dakimbo.

"I don't care if he's the star of Bethlehem. I'm not going to have my sons associating with this rude young man."

"You signed a contract."

I stood straight in a defiant posture, chin up, folded arms. "Sue me."

Mr Dakimbo was obviously heated—his face tightened, nostrils flared. "Mr Trout, I would like to have a word with you...alone."

"Where my daddy goes, we go," Headley said firmly.

Fred agreed with a thumbs up and then Mildead nodded, setting her arm around my shoulder.

"You see, Mr Dakimbo. What concerns me concerns my family."

"Fine."

Mr Dakimbo led us outside of the conference room into the hallway. His demeanour immediately took a 180-degree turn. "Listen to me, Mr Trout. You signed a contract. And you and your boys will honour that contract. Or else...."

"Or else, what?"

Fred and Headley pushed their way between Mr Dakimbo and me, looking straight up.

"Yeah. Or else, what?"

The studio head lowered his eyes to my boys and said, "You will see what I am capable of."

Fred wagged his finger and then Headley snapped, "No. You will see what we're capable of."

"Mr Dakimbo, our business with you is finished. We'll see ourselves out." I reached down and grabbed Fred's hand. "Come on, boys. Let's go."

Fred pulled his hand away from me and raised his fists at Mr Dakimbo, like a bare-knuckle fighter. I snatched his hand back and pulled him and his brother away from the large studio head who snarled back at them. Fred countered with a slap on his own butt and the raising of his favourite finger.

Back in our car, we drove up to the studio lot gate to exit, but the guard slid his window open and held us up with the show of his palm.

"Did you find everything all right?" asked the guard through the open window.

"We found everything, all right," I said. "But it wasn't pretty."

The security guard, a middle-aged Mexican American, leaned further out of the window a few inches. "What do you mean?"

"Your boss was a jerk. And he threatened us with an 'or-else' remark if we didn't honour our contract."

Lowering his voice, the security guard muttered, "There's been talk among some of the employees that Mr Dakimbo isn't who he says he is."

I leaned further out of my car window. "Oh, yeah?"

"Uh-huh. They say Mr Dakimbo is really Abasi Uba, the former president of Sierra Leone, who'd embezzled tons of money and took off, coming here."

"Oh, really? But is there proof."

The security guard scanned the area before reaching into his pocket and taking out a folded newspaper clipping.

"Take a look at this. A co-worker of mine gave it to me."

I unfolded the newspaper clipping, and there was a photo of a man who looked exactly like MrDakimbo entering a vehicle. The headline of the article read: President Abasi Uba Flees Sierra Leone.

I read the entire article, and it indeed stated that Abasi Uba had embezzled money and fled, most likely to America. I showed the clipping to Mildead and the boys.

"That's him, daddy. I'm sure of it," said Headley.

"I'm sure of it, too." I took back the newspaper clipping from my son and gave it back to the security guard.

The security guard raised his eyebrows. "How about that for proof? My boss is a straight-up criminal."

"Why did you tell us all this," I asked, "and show us the clipping?"

"I'm quitting anyway... on my last week. So are a few other employees. I don't feel right working here any longer."

"Okay. Good for you. I hope you find a better job. And thanks for the information."

I parked the car in the parking lot of a nearby shopping mall. I wanted to talk to my family about Mr Dakimbo. We were here to punish and eat bad people and criminals. I didn't want us to forget why we came to Los Angeles.

I swivelled to the side, facing Mildead and the boys. "Okay, guys. You all want to eat Mr Dakimbo's brain?"

"Yeah!" shouted Mildead and Headley while Fred clapped.

"All right. Let's get to it...Oh, boys. I'm sorry about your movie deal. I didn't like that kid making fun of you. He was mean spirited."

"Daddy, let's eat him, too. He'd been in jail for assaulting the mayor," said Headley, smiling.

"Okay," I sputtered, "Mildead?"

Mildead hit me with one of those do-you-really-have-to-ask looks.

"Sorry. Never mind. Let's go eat us a big bad African and a bratty white boy!"

"Daddy, are you going to eat them, too?" Headley asked enthusiastically.

I gave my son one of that 'am-I-a-zombie?' looks.

"Oops. Sorry, daddy."

I drove my little family back toward the Independent Studios' parking lot. When we got there, we cruised around the block a few times until a parking space freed up right across the street from the studio lot. Perfect. I didn't want to park in the lot and get logged in as a visitor. We had left earlier, so we were already logged out.

"All right, family, we're on an old fashion stakeout," I said.

"Mr Lipshitz had said the meet and greet would last no more than two hours. We had left around a half-hour ago.

I'm pretty sure that so-called pop star will be the first to leave that meeting. Keep a lookout."

While my family were keeping an eye out on the studio gate, I gazed at my two boys and thought how much I loved them. They are my heroes... everything I always wanted to be, my mind sang. I smiled as I watched Fred rub his hands together and unconsciously lift his right foot then the left foot, anxious and determined to take on all evildoers. He was bold, athletic, and didn't take any crap from anyone, even from me. He's got to work on that last one, I muttered softly to myself. And Headley, my little general, didn't even blink, as he focused on that studio gate. My two geniuses, my fearless enforcers. They were my alter ego.

"What's that swishing noise?" I asked to no one in particular.

Headley turned his head to me. "Oh, that's Fred and his corduroy pants."

"Oh."

Fred raised both hands and clapped.

"Daddy, someone is coming out of the gate," Headley reported.

A silver Range Rover pulled out of the studio lot and drove right by us.

"I didn't see who it was through the tinted windows," I said.

"Daddy, it's Dustin."

"How do you know?"

"Because of his license plate, 2Cool4U. That's the name of his first hit song."

"All right. I'm on him."

I put the Pacer into drive and hung a u-ey in the middle of the street. The Range Rover was a half a block ahead of us.

"Dang, that kid drives fast," I expressed.

"Daddy, he's within the speed limit at thirty miles per hour. You're only going twenty."

"Not for long, baby." I floored the accelerator.

"Okay, daddy, now you're at twenty-five miles per hour. Kick it into gear!"

We were now right behind him.

I smirked. "We got that sucker! Try to outrun me, huh!"

"Daddy, we're coming up at a red light. That's why he slowed down."

"Oh, okay. Good. You guys know what to do, right?"

One and all nodded.

"All right, here we go."

At the stoplight, I pressed down on the accelerator and rear-ended the Range Rover, damaging the rear bumper. In an instant, Dustin Beaver shot out of his vehicle and stormed my way. My little family then exited the Pacer, drifting away from the upcoming confrontation.

Before Dustin stepped up to my car, he glanced at his rear bumper.

"Damn!" Looking furious, he came to me.

"Oh, I'm sorry, young man," I said, rolling down my window.

"What the hell! It's you! Look what ya did to my Rover, ya old four-eye fool!" Dustin ranted.

"Hey, I'm in my prime at thirty-two years of age, thank you very much. If you hadn't slammed on your brakes, I wouldn't have hit you. Therefore, you caused the accident, young man" I hated lying, but somehow I was getting better at it.

"Me! You daft, OG. I was already stopped at the light."

"You shouldn't tell fibs, young man. Your mother wouldn't like it."

"Don't talk about my momma! Get outta the car!" Dustin pulled on the car door handle, but it was locked.

"Hey, you better cool it, kid. I'm a black belt in kung fu."

"Kung fu doesn't use belts, Butt Crack."

"My kung fu does." I whipped off my belt from my pants and unlocked the door, pushing it open. I stood up and whirled the belt in the air, forcing Dustin to back up.

Dustin held his hands up. "Okay, chill, OG. Let's just exchange info...insurance and whatever."

"I don't have insurance," I confessed. "You better get back in your car, or I'm gonna give you a whippin' that you certainly deserve."

"Oh, I gotta weapon, too, OG. A 9mm. Wait here, fool." Dustin Beaver headed back toward his car to get his gun from the glove department. When he hopped up into the Range Rover, his face stretched from shock. In the passenger seat, were Fred and Headley who sat on Mildead's lap.

Headley smiled wickedly. "Hello, Dustin. Will you join us for dinner?"

My little family chomped on the pop star's brain with much delight. They soon dumped the rest of the body in the back of the Range Rover, covering it with a bunch of the teen's own clothes that were stuffed in a duffel bag. I told Mildead to drive the Range Rover and follow me to the city of Compton.

I had to keep a close eye on Mildead through the rear-view mirror—her driving record was highly unreliable and suspect.

Later, we arrived at a narrow alley, a few blocks away from Gloria and Winston's house. I instructed Mildead to leave the keys in the Range Rover, put down all the windows, and leave the doors unlocked. Then my little family scooted in the Pacer.

"Why did we leave the keys in the Range Rover, daddy," Headley asked.

"A brand new car like that in gang territory is bound to be stolen by some punk. And hey, if it does get stolen, hopefully, that punk gets stopped by the cops while Dustin's dead body is in the back.

We'll definitely kill two stones with one flying bird, baby."

"It's killing two birds with one stone, daddy."

"Really? But your grandmother had always said two stones, one flying bird."

"Take my word for it, daddy."

We left the Range Rover in the alley and went over to my nephew's house. There was no one at home, so we decided to return to Independent Studios to finish our business with the big African.

Might as well kill two flies with one gallstone, I said to myself, feeling smart. Mildead and the boys were game. They could eat brains all day. I just wanted to get Mr Dakimbo or whatever his name was, out of the way as quick as possible. I didn't want the police to find Dustin's body and start asking questions around the film studio.

It wasn't all that difficult to get back into the studio lot—the security guard waved us in with no questions asked—he didn't even log us back in. I guess he was going to make his last week at work an easy one. The armed security guard, outside MD Headquarters, barely glanced at us as we entered the double doors. It was always refreshing not to get typecast as a threat to one's safety.

Through the long corridor, we came upon the conference room and peered through the glass windows. No one was there.

I knocked on MrDakimbo's office door. There was no answer. I slid opened the door and stuck my head inside, scanning the office. I didn't see anyone, but then I heard a toilet flush.

Mr Dakimbo's private restroom was located at the rear of the office, behind a secret door that was made to look like a large bookcase that was ajar. My little family and I invited ourselves in and sneaked our way toward the bookcase door. As I slowly pushed the door wide open, Mildead and the boys stood at the entrance, staring at Mr Dakimbo doing his thing on the toilet. I moved between Mildead and my sons and joined in the poop watching.

"Hey, Abasi Uba!" My voice was loud and clear.

The studio head snapped to attention, raising his head, and he slammed his back against the toilet tank. As soon as he saw who it was, his eyes glared, and his lips and fists tightened. "What the hell are you doing here! Who let you in my office?"

I let the big African have it, showing a wide grin. "Nobody was around, so we took the liberty to sightsee in your office. But we may have seen too much. I'd never seen another adult take a crap before."

"My two personal guards weren't outside my office?"

"Nope."

The studio head was livid. "Damn, Oyebo and Kojo. They are always taking breaks together. I keep telling them to take their breaks alone while the other stands guard. And wait a minute... How do you know my real name?"

"So, you are in fact Abasi Uba," I said, "the former president of Sierra Leone who embezzled millions of dollars."

"What business is it of yours?"

Fred signed a response and Headley translated, "Abasi Uba. You are a criminal and a thief. We hereby sentence you to death. Do you have any last words before we eat your brain?"

"Eat my what?"

Headley looked up at me and said, "Daddy, those were his last words. May we?"

"Yes, you may."

I turned away as Mildead, and the boys walked ominously toward the studio head. I wasn't into seeing blood and brain residue splattering all over the place. I was going to have to talk to my zombie family to see if they could find a way to eat brains without making so much of mess, I said to myself.

Abasi Uba held up his hands. "Wait! You people are joking, right?"

"No. They're zombies," I said as my back was turned.

(My Zombie Family: Fugitives of the Law)

James T. Fenimore awoke to find Sodead and Toodead feeling the top of his head.

"Hey, cut that out!" barked James, swiping the sisters' hands away. "What were you two doing?"

"We just wanted to see if you had a well-shaped head. There's no way to tell with all that curly hair you have." Toodead's reply was flimsy.

"I know you two were sizing up my head to see if I had a big brain. No more touching. Is that clear?"

"Fine," said Toodead, who quickly folded her arms.

From the passenger seat, Sodead smiled and reached over Toodead, pointing a teasing finger at James, nearly touching his arm—a half-inch away.

James pulled out his twelve-inch hunting knife from under his windbreaker jacket and showed it to Sodead. "Do it and lose it."

"I was just having fun with you, J.T.," Sodead protested. "Don't be so serious. Anyway, you may get one of us but not both of us. You better believe that."

"Look, I'm here helping you, ladies. I just don't want to get touched, okay."

Sodead withdrew to her seat, sitting forward, eyes ahead. "Fine with me."

James unhooked his cell phone from his carrying case that was attached to his belt. "I'm going to call this number that was on the boys' resume or whatever you call it." He reached into his pocket and took out a partially torn sheet of paper, unfolding it. Then he pressed eleven numbers on his phone. A few seconds later, someone answered his call.

"Hello, can I speak to Filmon Trout, please," James said clearly.

"Don't tell him we're here," whispered Toodead

James nodded and whispered back, "It sounds like a little kid," then he returned to his phone conversation, "Who am I? I'm James T. Feni..." James paused—he didn't want to say his real name, "uh...James Tefeni. That's right, James Tefeni.... What's my business with your father? I'm a ... uh...his coworker...What kind of job do I do? I'm a...what's with all the questions? I just want to talk with your father. Okay, I'll answer your question. I'm a..."

"A Wildlife Waste Handler," Toodead whispered again.

James continued, "I'm a Wild Wife Weight Handler. I—"

"No. A Wildlife Waste Handler," Toodead repeated, slapping James on the shoulder.

"I mean ...uh, Wild Eye Waste Hater..."

Toodead slapped his shoulder even harder.

"Ow... Hello? Are you still there?" James turned to Mildead. "The little brat hung up."

"I said Wildlife Waste Handler," Toodead enunciated loud and clear.

"You were whispering. I couldn't hear you properly. I'll call him again."

"Never mind. That was Filmon's son, Headley. He won't answer it again...too smart. It's hard to fool him. Too bad his father hadn't answered it—he'll fall for anything."

"What do we do now?" said Sodead to her sister.

Toodead looked to James, wanting him to answer instead.

James caught Toodead's gaze and said, "We'll just have to wait until they show up."

Back at Independent Studios, Hollywood homicide detectives Philip Lee and Leslie Vera had just arrived at the crime scene of the murdered studio head Matumbe Dakimbo, whose headless body was propped up on a toilet seat. Already at the scene were six police officers who were securing the area, and a man wearing a grey suit, sifting through the evidence with tweezers. The two detectives drifted toward the man and stood behind him.

"Excuse me, who are you?" asked detective Lee. The man rose from squatting and turned around. He then reached in the inner pocket of his blazer and pulled out his badge and identification card, showing them to the detectives. "My name is special agent Walters, Central Intelligence Agency."

Detective Lee glanced at his partner then moved his eyes back to the CIA agent. "I'm confused.

Aren't you out of your jurisdiction, special agent Walters?"

"And who are you?"

"I'm detective Lee, and my partner here is detective Vera, homicide."

Agent Walters offered an obligatory nod and said, "The agency has been closely observing MrDakimbo's movements ever since he arrived in the states. His real name is Abasi Uba, the former president of Sierra Leone."

"I've heard of him. He embezzled millions of dollars after selling off a lot of that country's resources to private corporations," said detective Vera, who then started to write the names of agent Walters and Abasi Uba in her notepad.

Detective Lee noticed agent Walters' well-tailored Italian wool-suit, admiring the man's taste. He then asked,

"What does the CIA have to do with Mr Dakimbo?"

"That, I cannot divulge. It's a matter of national security."

Detective Lee let out an exasperated sigh—he had a feeling agent Walters was going to bring up national security. "Well, since you were here first, have you found anything interesting or unusual pertaining to this homicide? I'm sure you can answer that."

The CIA agent nodded. "Mr Dakimbo's brain was removed from his head and possibly eaten.

Also, there are two different sizes of bite marks all over his upper body. One set seemed to have been made by a child."

"A child?" detective Lee snapped back.

"I believe so. Take a look for yourself." Agent Walters turned around and stepped toward the studio head's dead body. He then pointed to the smaller set of bite marks on the victim's chest. "See here how significantly smaller these bite marks are. And what's more interesting, look at these distinctive impressions...as if the biter had fangs."

"Vera, call in to get a forensic dentist here, right away," directed detective Lee.

As detective Vera took out her cell phone from her coat pocket, a police officer knocked on the open bathroom door, and standing behind him, was one of Mr Dakimbo's security guards.

Detective Lee stood straight and acknowledged the officer's presence with a head nod.

The police officer stepped to the side and gestured for the security guard to stand at the doorway.

"Sir, this is the victim's security guard. He may have some pertinent information."

A young West African with a working visa, the security guard, cleared his throat before he said, "There was a family that entered the building after a few of Mr Dakimbo's guests had left.

The family was here earlier, then returned. I believe they were the last to see Mr Dakimbo alive."

"Do you have them on your security cameras?" Detective Lee asked.

"Yes, we do. And they are also in a commercial."

"Commercial? What type of commercial?"

"A Head & Shoulders commercial."

Detective Lee had his partner look up the commercial on YouTube.

After getting off the phone from calling a forensic dentist, detective Vera YouTubed the Head & Shoulders commercial. When she found it, she handed her smartphone to detective Lee. '

'Check this out."

The middle-aged detective had a look of astonishment. "Is that a real kid?"

"Very real. I saw them with my own eyes," the security guard declared.

"Them?"

"Those are two boys. One of them doesn't have a head.

Detective Lee grew silent, taking in what he had just heard with scepticism. Then, with his eyes still on the security guard, he allowed agent Walters to watch the commercial.

"How does one survive without a head?"

The security guard shrugged his shoulders.

Agent Walters lifted his sights from the smartphone and spoke to the security guard, "Did the parents enter here with their sons?"

"Yes."

"Then I believe we have our prime suspects," agent Walters said, as he handed the smartphone back to detective Vera.

Detective Lee's scepticism still lingered. "How do you figure that?"

"The commercial. Didn't you see the little boy smile? His canines were pointed, not wide and blunt like yours and mine. I'm sure his teeth match the bite marks on the body."

Agent Walters walked by the two detectives then pivoted. "Detective Lee, I need two uniformed officers to help me confiscate all files and computer disks from Mr Uba's office."

He took out a business card from his wallet and offered it to the detective.

"This is the number of the agency's branch office here in Los Angeles. If there are any doubts about my presence, I suggest you call that number."

He had failed to mention the CIA branch office was a mobile one, moving from city to city.

Detective Lee held up his hand and immediately called the number on his cell phone. After being redirected three times, he finally connected to the Directorate of Operations office, the clandestine arm of the CIA. He nodded a few times then frowned. He put the phone back in his coat pocket and walked to the bathroom's entrance. He then called out for two uniformed police officers to assist agent Walters.

"Thank you, detective," agent Walters said, hiding a smirk.

While detectives Lee and Vera examined more of the crime scene, agent Walters was in Mr Dakimbo's office, studying Fred and Headley's revamped acting bio that was under Dustin Beaver's bio, atop a filing cabinet. He wasn't interested in catching the studio head's killers. All he wanted was any information linking the former Sierra Leone President to the CIA or the Chinese government. As the two uniformed officers were dumping all types of paperwork in boxes, agent Walters covertly took out Fred and Headley's bio and headshot from the folder and folded the items, slipping them in his inside coat pocket, just in case he would need them for future references.

Jeremy Walters, a double agent, loyally spied for the CIA for three years until he learned that the Chinese government was an extravagant contributor to the cash-for-information trade. For the past six years, he had sold vital and not so vital information to the Chinese who regarded any classified material from the United States as necessary information. He had brokered a deal with the CIA's Deputy Director for Intelligence, to give Abasi Uba sanctuary in the United States, and in return, have the former Sierra Leone president keep open communications with the Chinese, divulging to the agency anything and everything. But the Director for Intelligence had no inclination that agent Walters, Abasi Uba, and the Chinese government were in cahoots against the United States.

Agent Walters had the two uniformed officers pack the back of his Jeep Wrangler, with two large boxes full of the studio head's computer disks and files. He hadn't informed detectives Lee and Vera about Fred and Headley's acting bio. He figured they would find the two suspects sooner or later. Before getting into his jeep, the CIA agent reached into his pocket and bought out the boys' bio, and something was bothering him. He felt that he wasn't covering all the bases. So he decided to call the number on the bio, checking if anyone answers. Maybe there was a connection between the killers and the Chinese government, or even the CIA, he thought.

As the CIA agent was calling, he began to wonder if his suspicion of the little boys, along with their parents being cannibalistic killers was folly. Yet there was enough circumstantial evidence pointing their way: the security guard's eyewitness account of the family entering the

building shortly before the murder and one of the boys'
fanglike teeth, which corresponded with the small bite
marks on the dead body. He promptly brushed off his
doubts just before someone answered his call, for it was
time to be a spy again.

(Family Reunion)

"Headley, who is it?" I asked as I drove toward our motel.

Headley held up a hand and spoke again into his cell phone, "No, this isn't Mr Trout. I won't be a mister until at least eighteen years of age. I'm Headley. Whom shall I say is calling?" Headley then nodded, and after several seconds he covered his cell phone. '

"Daddy, it's a reporter from the Los Angeles Herald. He saw Fred and me in our commercial. He wants to interview us."

"Really? That's great. Oh, do you boys want to do it?"

Fred raised two thumbs.

"Cool," smiled Headley.

I asked him when.

"Wait, is the reporter here?"

"Yes, daddy."

"Ask him when and where does he want to meet?"

Headley did what he was told, and then he replied back to me, "The reporter said that you should pick the time and place at your convenience."

"Okay, give him our motel address—"

"Daddy, don't you want the cell phone, to tell him the address?"

"I'm driving, son."

"Oh, yeah."

I paused, losing my train of thought for a moment—too much excitement, and then I told Headley to give the reporter our motel address, room number, and two hours for a meeting time, so to give us with enough time to get back to the motel to change our bloodstained clothes and then shower.

"He said fine, daddy. He'll be at the motel in two hours," Headley reported.

"All right, great. Now, as soon as we get back to the motel, we hit the shower."

Out of the corner of my eye, I saw Fred signing, but I didn't catch it.

"What was that, Fred?"

Headley twisted his mouth, obviously unhappy.

"Fred said that he's got first dibs on the shower. He always gets to shower first, daddy."

It's so cute how Headley often forgets that he's connected to his brother, I thought, smiling.

Sodead hit her sister on the arm, after seeing Filmon's orange Pacer park right in front of James' van.

"There they are."

"How do you know it's them?" said James.

"Not too many people in the world have an orange 1978 Pacer with a bumper sticker that reads, 'Proud to be a Wildlife Waste Handler.'"

James and the two sisters kept their attention on Filmon as his family got out of the Pacer and walked toward their motel room.

James felt anxious and asked, "what do we do? Follow them to their room?"

"No. We need to get Filmon alone, away from Mildead and the boys," Toodead replied, with her eyes still on the Trout family.

"All right. Should we try to come up with another plan?"

Toodead reverted her gaze from Filmon and his family to James.

"No. Your first plan was good enough. Just do what you did before. Knock on their room door and persuade Filmon to come with you back here to the van. And once he's near the van's side door, my sister and I will pull him inside."

"Ooh goody," Sodead said, rubbing her hands together.

James was excited about aiding in the next kill, but he was practical when it came to his work. "I think we should wait until it gets dark before we make our move."

"No way," Sodead protested, "I'm hungry for Filmon's brain now. We've been waiting for hours. I can't wait any longer."

"Look, I don't do any killing in the daytime. We could easily get spotted."

Sodead dismissed James' comment with a muffled tight-lipped exhale. "You won't be doing the killing. My sister and I will do it. Just lead him to us, you Ted Bundy wannabe."

"You better watch it," James snarled, pointing a stiff finger. "There's an artistic technique that I put forth in my kills. Ted Bundy was a crude killer. I'm more subtle and clean."

"Yeah, right."

"Whatever. And I'm serious. We'll wait until nighttime or no time."

Sodead tightened her lips and raised herself from off the seat.

"Sodead, sit back down," growled Toodead, who hit her sister on the shoulder. "He's right. The night is better. We'll wait until then."

Sodead held her shoulder and whined, "You hit me. You've never hit me before, even when we were alive."

Toodead softly rubbed her sister's shoulder. "I'm sorry, my dear sister. But you can be rash at times. We'll soon eat Filmon's brain, but we need to be more practical and cautious."

With a bent finger, Sodead knocked on Toodead's head three times. "Hellooo. We're zombies, for goodness sakes. We're not programmed to be practical and cautious."

Toodead swivelled slowly toward Sodead and glared at her. "Don't ever do that again. And, we're waiting until it gets dark. That's final."

Sodead slammed her back against the seat, huffing and puffing. She knew to keep silent when her sister spoke harshly.

"Daddy, someone's at the door!" yelled Headley.

"Well, answer it!" I yelled back from inside the bathroom, washing my hands.

"I can't, Fred's doing pushups!"

"Fred, answer the door!"

"He's not stopping until he hits thirty pushups, daddy!"

I quickly dried my hands and rushed out of the bathroom. As I was passing Fred doing his pushups, Headley shrugged his shoulders and silently mouthed an apology.

"Fred, you could've interrupted your pushups to answer the door."

Fred replied with a bursting fart.

"Whatever, Fred," I said before opening the front door.

A man stood at the doorway, wearing dark sunglasses. He was a bit taller than me, around six-foot-two inches, and he had a scruffy face like he hadn't shaved in a week. But he wore a nice grey suit that contrasted with his scruffiness. He took his sunglasses off before speaking.

"Mr Trout?" the man said.

"Yeah. Are you the reporter?"

"Yes. Hello, my name is Carter Haynes of the Los Angeles Herald. I'm writing a piece on extraordinary children. And your two boys are extraordinary. When I saw them in that commercial, I was just stunned by their talent, especially their uniqueness."

I grinned, already liking the guy. "That's what I keep telling my boys. They're unique. Come on in, Mr Haynes."

"Thank you."

Fred and Headley, along with Mildead, were now sitting on one of two double beds, watching a Brady Bunch rerun on television. As Mr Haynes and I stood at the foot of the empty bed, Mildead nodded a greeting, but the boys were too engrossed, singing along with the Brady kids.

"Fred... Headley..." I tried to get their attention, but they kept on singing.

"♪We're gonna keep on, keep on, keep on, keep on dancing all through the night. We're gonna keep on, keep on, keep on doing it right.♪"

"Boys!" I called out. Finally, I got their attention.

"Oh, sorry, daddy," answered Headley.

Fred was still moving to the music.

"Fred!"

Fred's body gradually became still, and then he gave us his attention with a twist of his body.

I made the introductions.

"Boys, this is Carter Haynes, the reporter from the Los Angeles Herald.

"Hello, Mr Haynes, I'm Headley."

Fred introduced himself by signing.

"Hello, Headley," Mr Haynes said. Then he greeted and introduced himself to Fred by also using sign language.

Fred clapped.

"Hey, Mr Haynes, you know sign language," I grinned.

"I just picked it up over the years." Mr Haynes gave everyone a thorough inspection with his eyes, and then he spoke to the boys, "Okay, Fred and Headley, are you two ready for the interview?"

"Oh, yeah," hummed Headley.

Fred raised two thumbs.

Mr Haynes nodded. "Good."

I grabbed a wooden chair that was near the bathroom door and offered it to Mr Haynes.

"Thank you." The Herald reporter sat down, and then he took out a notepad from his coat pocket. "All right, Fred and Headley, I'd heard you both were signed on to do a film for Independent Studios."

"Yeah, Mahatma Zombie," said Headley. "We were to play zombie spies, but we decided not to do the movie."

"Why?"

"That Mr Dakimbo was a real jerk. I'm glad we ate his—"

"Headley!" I said, raising my voice.

"Yes, daddy?"

I couldn't believe my son—big brain, big mouth. "We...we hadn't eaten yet, remember?" I had to get the boy off of ratting us out.

"Huh?"

I shot my son a laser beam eye, sending him a don't-say-we-ate-Mr Dakimbo's brain signal.

Headley thought deeply for a moment and then nodded, finally getting my signal. "Oh, yeah, that's right, daddy. We...ate...already."

Mr Haynes kept to his questions, "So, Headley. Mr Dakimbo was a jerk, huh?"

Headley glanced at me before replying, "Just say he'd rather have a...uh..."

Fred signed quickly.

"Yeah, a butthole brat as the main actor who speaks rudely and disrespectfully to others, especially to my brother and I. We can't associate with anyone who allows bad manners to run rampant in the workplace."

The Herald reporter was taken aback by Headley's use of words. "How old are you, Headley?"

"My brother and I just turned two years old. Fred's older by around five minutes or so."

Mr Haynes raised his eyebrows and drooped his head forward, surprised by Headley's answer.

"Two?"

"Yep. My daddy says that my brother and I are geniuses, but we don't feel like we are."

"Well, you two are certainly just that," confirmed Mr Haynes. "Okay, I want to hear more about your relationship with Mr Dakimbo. Have you boys worked with him on any other projects?"

Headley shook his head, and Fred wagged a finger.

"Have you ever visited Africa?"

Fred shook his head again and a wagged finger.

Mr Haynes wrote on his notepad, and then he returned to question the boys.

"Do you have any...affiliation with the Chinese government?"

"No. But I'm going to learn Mandarin pretty soon," Headley said proudly.

"Excuse me, Mr Haynes. I...I'm not sure if those questions are relevant to the boys' work as actors," I said.

"I believe the questions are relevant. Your sons may someday have fans from Africa and China."

I puffed out my chest, proud of the possibility my boys may be international stars. "You know, I believe the questions are relevant. Sorry for questioning your expertise in reporting."

"Oh, nothing to be sorry for."

While Mr Haynes and I had been talking, I peeked at Fred digging in his rear pants pocket. He had brought out a folded sheet of paper, unfolded it, and had Headley read it in silence.

"What are you boys reading?" Mr Haynes asked.

"Oh, it's just a souvenir from Mr Dakimbo's office," Headley said.

Mr Haynes' eyes stretched wide. "Can I see it?"

Headley looked to his brother for permission, and then Fred gave a thumbs up.

"Hey, wait. Let me—" I was too late to check what was on the sheet of paper—Fred had already handed it to Mr Haynes.

Headley went on to explain the paper's contents, "It's just a bunch of names of people and names of companies. It even has bank account numbers with cash amounts next to them. There was a name in parenthesis on the bottom of the page, a Jeremy Walters. Then the letters CIA and MSS. I memorised every word."

Mr Haynes was silent—his attention never wavered from the sheet of paper. He seemed dumbfounded, and his face was pale like he was in a state of shock.

"Mr Haynes, are you all right?" I asked.

"What?"

"Are you all right?"

"Oh, yeah. I...I'm fine. I—"

"Mr Haynes," said Headley, "I know what CIA stands for, but I don't know what MSS is. I'm going to Google it."

With his eyes still on the sheet of paper, Mr Haynes muttered, "Ministry of State Security. China's intelligence agency."

"Cool," breathed Headley. "Then that Jeremy Walters must be a double agent or something, working for the CIA and the MSS.

The Herald Reporter broke out of his semi-stupor and asked.

"Why do you say that?"

"That happens all the time with spies, being double agents or selling off national secrets. So many books and movies about it."

Mr Haynes held up the sheet of paper, near the side of his head and asked, "Fred, is this the only copy?"

Fred flicked up a thumb.

"Can I keep this?"

Fred wagged a finger.

"I'll give you five dollars for it."

Fred pointed an index finger toward the ceiling.

"Ten dollars?"

Fred pointed two index fingers in the air.

Mr Haynes seemed vexed.

"Okay, twenty dollars."

Fred folded his arms and paused for a few seconds. Then he raised his hand and tapped Headley on the shoulder.

Headley smiled at Mr Haynes and said, "Fred wants one million dollars."

The Herald reporter chuckled. "Fred, you're kidding, right?'

Fred wagged two index fingers.

Mr Haynes had a look of exasperation. "All right, I'm tired of beating around the bush." The reporter reached into his coat for something, but he suddenly froze when someone knocked on the door.

"I'll answer it," I said, but not before giving Mr Haynes a sideways glance for his odd comment.

I opened the door, and standing in front of me was a huge offensive-tackle of man who showed me a friendly smile.

"Excuse me, sir. Do you own an orange Pacer?" the large man asked.

"Yes, I do. Why do you ask?"

"Dang, little brats. Thanks for telling me." I turned around and faced my kids. "Boys, I'm going see about my car."

"I wanna go too, daddy. Hold up," mouthed Headley, who then spoke to his brother, "Fred, you wanna go?"

Fred gave his brother a thumbs up and hopped off the bed with Headley in tow. Fred then moved toward Mr Haynes, snatched the sheet of paper out of the reporter's hand, and headed for the door.

"Sorry, Mr Haynes. But we gotta postpone the interview," Headley said. "We got some butt kicking to do. Come on, Mommy."

Mildead immediately followed her sons.

As I waited at the doorway for my little family, I thought I had seen Mr Haynes set a gun back in its holster. I quickly convinced myself that I was just seeing things. I gotta get new glasses, I thought.

The large man and I walked briskly, side by side toward my car, as Mildead and the boys were a few steps ahead.

"Sir, you don't need your whole family to confront those kids. You and I could handle them," said the large man.

"Where I go, my family goes. Anyway, my boys are the muscle of the family.... What's your name?"

"James."

"My name is Filmon Trout. Thanks again."

"Your boys are...a...unique looking, Filmon."

"That's what I keep telling them," I said smiling.

When we came upon my Pacer, there were no teens anywhere near the car.

"I guess those vandalizing criminals took off before we were going to kick their butts," Headley rumbled.

"There they go, around the corner!" Yelled James, pointing toward the end of the block.

I looked to where James was pointing, but I didn't see anyone.

James turned to Mildead and the boys. "Why don't you three go after them around the corner, and Filmon and I will head them off this way." James jerked a head nod toward the opposite direction of where he had said he'd seen the teens run away.

"James, I think we should just let them go. Anyway, my car doesn't seem to be damaged."

"They may have taken something from inside your car," James countered.

"I don't think I had anything of value in the car."

Headley spoke after clearing his throat. "Daddy, what about your 8-track tape of the Partridge Family?"

After my eyes widened, I darted to the Pacer and swung the passenger door open. I then rummaged through the glove compartment but couldn't find my Partridge Family 8-track tape.

"Bastards." I got out of the car and faced my family. "My Partridge Family tape isn't there!"

Fred caught my attention as he signed a comment.

"Son, I don't remember taking the tape inside the house. I may have, but I can't take that chance. Let's get those thievin' brats."

"Yeah!" a gung-ho Headley shouted.

James smirked before saying,

"Boys, you and your mother go that way. And your father and I will go this way."

Mildead and the boys took off running.

James patted me on the back. "Come on, Filmon."

"Yep. Let's get 'em."

James started to trot, but he stopped abruptly. He then walked up to a van and opened the side door. "Filmon, first I gotta get something from my van. Can you give me a hand with something?"

"Sure."

"My back is hurting me.... Uh, I can't bend over so much. Filmon, can you go inside the van and hand me a large bag while I stand out here?"

"No problem." I stepped inside the van and looked for a large bag. "It's kinda dark in here." I then suddenly heard a familiar voice.

"Hello, Filmon." Toodead winked with a smile.

"Hi, Filmon," smirked Sodead.

I gulped hard when I saw Mildead's sisters. And then the van's side door slammed shut. Not only was I frightened, I was confused.

"What are you two doing in Los Angeles?"

"We're here to see you, Filmon," returned Toodead.

I put on a fake smile and said,

"Okay, you saw me. It was good seeing you girls. Gotta go." As soon as I turned to open the side door, Toodead grabbed my arm and held it tight.

"Don't be such in a hurry, Filmon," said Toodead. "We haven't seen you in awhile. We missed you."

Sodead snatched up my other arm and started to pull me back. "Yeah, we missed you. Didn't you miss us?"

"Not really. Please, let me go before I karate chop the both of you."

Toodead and Sodead eyed each other, and both began to giggle.

"I didn't know you knew Karate, Filmon," said Toodead, who winked at her sister.

"Hi-ya!" I yelled.

The two sisters once again gave each other the eye and then laughed.

While half laughing, Toodead said, "Filmon, why...why did you just say 'Hi-ya', with ...without doing anything?"

An uneasy feeling edged out my fears.

"Well, since you two were holding my arms, I thought I'd scare you both with just my karate yell."

"You make me laugh, Filmon. I may regret it a little when I eat your brain."

"Not me," Sodead added.

"Hey, wait a minute! My...my brain isn't as tasty as you might think. It's a bit fried. You zombies like your brains fresh and rare."

Sodead licked her lips.

"Oh, your brain will be so delicious."

I had to think of something quickly, so I turned and nodded at the front windshield, and then I bluffed, "Look! It's the King of England!"

Toodead and Sodead never took their eyes off of me, not falling for my bluff.

Dammit!

Toodead snickered.

"Good try, Filmon."

Sodead began to pull me closer to her. "Now, it's time to eat."

"I already ate!"

James opened the driver side door and spouted off, "Hey, don't eat him here. Let's take him to a more secluded area."

A sudden hard thump hit the side of the van. Then the van's side door tore open.

"Everybody, Freeze!" bellowed Agent Walters, pointing a gun.

"Mr Haynes! Thank goodness!" I cried out, relieved.

"Mr Trout, come outside."

"I can't. They're holding me."

Agent Walters aimed his gun at Toodead and then at Sodead. "Let go of him, or I will shoot each of you in the head."

The van's engine erupted.

"Hey, turn off that engine!" Agent Walters shouted, now pointing his gun at the driver.

James stepped on the gas pedal, propelling the van forward, sideswiping my Pacer. Agent Walters shot at James twice, hitting only the windshield and driver side window as the van sped off toward Hollywood boulevard.

"You hit my car!" I yelled.

"Shut up!" James yelled back.

"You owe me for damages."

James glared at me from the rearview mirror. "When we're outta this city, you'll get paid, all right."

"Thank you." I then caught Toodead and Sodead's hungry eyes, feasting back at me. Dammit!

CHAPTER 17

(Help!)

Agent Walters stood on the sidewalk; eyes transfixed on the van's rear license plate, in which he promptly memorized. As he was about to cross the street to get to his car, he heard Headley's voice.

"Mr Haynes, have you seen my daddy?"

"He was just kidnapped. They took off in that van." Agent Walters pointed to the fleeing van that was three blocks away.

After Headley watched the van turn at a corner, he frantically cried, "Le...let's go after them! Do you have a car?"

"I have a car. But going after your father is none of my business."

Headley's eyes seared at the agent.

Then Fred took out the sheet of paper from his back pocket and showed it to agent Walters.

Headley's glare softened.

"Back in the motel room, you seemed very interested in this sheet of paper, Mr Haynes. If you take us with you to get our daddy back, Fred will give it to you."

Agent Walters opened his coat, revealing his holstered handgun. "What if I just take that piece of paper."

Headley's glare returned, then he showed his fangs. "Go ahead and try it, Mr Haynes. But as soon as you reach for that gun, I'll be munching on your brain."

The CIA agent remembered the ghastly remains of Abasi Uba sitting on the toilet. He knew Headley was capable of carrying out his threat. He closed up his coat, straightened his tie, and smiled.

"Let's go get your father."

Fred and Headley returned to being regular kids and raised their arms.

"Yay!"

"Okay, give me the piece of paper."

Fred wagged his finger.

"You'll get it when we get our daddy back," said Headley.

Agent Walters nodded, and he quickly led Mildead and the boys to his car.

***

Detectives Lee and Vera sat in a white unmarked Ford Crown Vic, surveilling agent Walters who was interacting with the child suspects. The homicide detectives hadn't been convinced of agent Walters' account of the studio head Matumbe Dakimbo's true identity. Mostly, they had been sceptical of the agent's presence at their crime scene. Detective Lee kept his focus on agent Walters, as his hunch that the CIA spook was up to something was growing steadily toward certainty. Quite often, his intuition was spot-on, and it seemed the detective's hunch had paid off again when the agent in question just gave the murder suspects in the Matumbe Dakimbo case a ride.

"What do you think is going on, Phil?" said detective Leslie Vera, who was driving the Crown Vic.

"I'm not sure. But I knew something wasn't right about that guy," detective Lee replied.

"He's driving pretty fast. You think he knows we're following him?"

"It's possible. Don't lose Walters."

***

Agent Walters squinted ahead while he drove on Hollywood boulevard, searching for the van.

"Do any of you see it?"

"There it is!" cried Headley.

"Where?"

"Up ahead, on the next block, right lane."

"That isn't the van. That one is black. The one we're looking for is dark blue."

Mildead, who was in the passenger seat, pointed and screamed.

"There!"

The CIA agent followed Mildead's pointed finger to a dark blue van driving on Highland ave. It was too late to turn right on Highland, for they were already in the middle of the intersection. Agent Walters glanced in the rearview mirror to see if there was a car behind him. When he saw that it was clear, he slammed on the brakes and put his Jeep Wrangler in reverse.

The Wrangler screeched backwards toward the beginning of the intersection, nearly crashing into a white Crown Vic. Agent Walters then spun his steering wheel to the right and stomped on the gas pedal, propelling his jeep north on Highland Avenue.

"That was cool!" Headley hailed. "Now, let's save my daddy!"

Agent Walters spotted the van, two blocks ahead. At the upcoming intersection, a traffic light was turning yellow.

"Punch it, Mr Haynes!" Headley shouted.

Agent Walters floored the gas pedal, and the Jeep Wrangler rocketed across the intersection amid honking and braking cars. Unbeknownst to the Wrangler's occupants, a white Crown Vic also crossed perilously through the intersection, close behind.

"Woo hoo!" Headley cried out, enjoying the ride.

It wasn't long before Agent Walters pulled his Jeep alongside the van and immediately noticed the gunshot hole in the passenger side window.

"Is that the right van, Mr Haynes?" asked Headley, who had his forehead pressed up against the window.

"Yes, it is," returned agent Walters, as he still had a watchful eye on the van.

"How are you going to stop the van? Maybe shoot out the tires?"

Agent Walters tilted his head and raised his eyebrows. "Not a bad idea. But I think I'm going to wait until we come upon a red light."

"And then we're gonna bum-rush the van, right?" Headley's voice was full of eagerness.

Agent Walters squinted at Headley through the rear-view mirror.

"Hey, are you sure you and your brother are only two years old?" He asked.

"Yep, that's right."

"I don't believe you."

Headley became incensed.

"Whaddya mean you don't believe me? Are you calling me a liar, MrHaynes?"

Agent Walters was caught off guard by Headley's heated reaction, and how the boy could shift from cute to hostile.

"Oh, no. I...I just never saw two-year-old kids as big as you and your brother. And how intelligent you both are."

Headley's cuteness returned with a smile.

"Well, my daddy says we're unique."

Agent Walters suddenly became serious and said, "I know you killed Mr Dakimbo."

"Yeah, he was rude. And, he was a thief," Headley muttered nonchalantly.

Mildead turned around from the front seat and shot her son a piercing eye.

Agent Walters noticed the traffic light up ahead just turned red, then he glanced at each family member and asked, "are you all in some type of cannibalistic cult?"

"Ew, gross," gagged Headley, "no way. My mom's a zombie. And Fred and I are half zombies."

Mildead sent her son a look of exhaustion.

Agent Walters scoffed inwardly, not believing one word from the boy. But he wasn't about to tell that to the quick-tempered Headley. He then saw that they were coming up at another red light.

"All right, as soon as I stop the car, I'm going to go over to the van and put my revolver to the driver's head. You all stay here."

"Oh, no, we aren't," argued Headley. "We're going, too. He's got our daddy."

The CIA agent wasn't going to argue. There was too little time.

"All right. But you three go to the other side of the van and open its side door. Your dad is in the back. And stay out of the line of fire."

"Cool!"

Fred had his hand on the door handle, ready to open the door as soon as agent Walters steps out of the jeep.

"Let's roll!" agent Walters roared.

Fred and Headley sprang out of the Jeep and cut around the van's rear while their mother followed at a brisk pace. With his gun lowered at his side, agent Walters crept up to the van's driver-side door and flung it open. He then shoved his weapon up against the driver's temple.

"If you press on the gas I'll put a bullet in the side of your head!" agent Walters growled. "Put it in park and get outta the vehicle!"

"All right! All right!" James yielded, setting the gear shift in park. He immediately raised his hands and stepped slowly out of the van.

Just as agent Walters slammed James up against the side of the van to frisk him, Mildead tore open the van's side door. Mildead's mouth gaped open when she laid her eyes upon her sisters holding her man

CHAPTER 18

(Family Love)

"Mildead!" I spouted. "It's not what you think. Your sisters kidnapped me."

Mildead nodded and smiled, "I know, Filmon."

"Daddy!" Headley howled, as his brother raised both arms.

I turned my head to leer at Sodead and Toodead. "Unhand me, demon sisters."

Headley raised a fist. "Yeah, let go of my daddy, beotches!"

"Headley, they're still your aunts! Have some respect!" I huffed sharply.

Headley frowned then said, "Sorry, aunty Sodead and aunty Toodead. Let go of my daddy, please."

Sodead and Toodead still held onto me until Mildead was about to set her foot in the van. Afraid of their older sister, the twins loosened their grips.

"Thank you," I said without any gratitude. Then, on my haunches, I slid out of from the side door and hugged and kissed my little family. I was so happy to see them.

All of a sudden men were shouting. My family and I immediately investigated the ruckus, creeping around the front of the van. We were shocked to see a man pointing a gun at Mr Haynes.

"Detective Lee, you're making a big mistake!" Mr Haynes' voice was full of conviction.

"Agent Walters, put your weapon down!" screamed detective Lee, who was alongside his partner, who also had her gun pointed at Mr Haynes and James.

"Hold up!" Mr Haynes fired back. "I'm apprehending a kidnapper here!"

"I said put your weapon down, agent Walters! I'm not going to repeat it!"

Still, at the front of the van, I turned to my family, a bit confused.

"Agent Walters?"

Fred signed quickly.

"Yeah, it's the same name of the CIA agent on your piece of paper," said Headley to Fred.

"You mean Mr Haynes is CIA agent Walters?" I said, surprised.

My son nodded back at me.

Agent Walters finally dropped his gun and then raised his arms. "You're making a big mistake, detective."

"Both of you, get down on your knees and place your hands behind your heads!"

James and the CIA agent promptly followed detective Lee's orders. With his gun still pointing at the two kneeling men, detective Lee mouthed off an order to his partner.

"Vera, check the passenger side for the others."

As detective Vera rounded the rear of the van, my family and I showed ourselves to the startled detective who took a few steps backwards.

"Hey, you three! Or...uh, four...whatever... Get over here and put your hands up!" shouted detective Lee. "And kneel alongside these two!"

We scrambled to kneel next to agent Walters and my abductor. I needed to clear up this misunderstanding.

"Excuse me, sir. I was just kidnapped. And I—"

"Shut the hell up and put your hands behind your head! That goes for all of you!"

"Hey, mister, don't talk like that to my daddy! He was kidnapped!" Headley heatedly responded.

"My name is detective Lee. And you shut up, too. You little fart."

Fred hopped up to his feet, and then Headley popped off. "Oh, no, he didn't!"

Detective Lee aimed his gun at my boys and shouted, "Get back on your knees!"

The sight of that detective pointing his gun at my two boys infuriated me.

"Yeah, no, he didn't!"

I rose to my feet and was about to tackle the detective, until a woman's scream pierced the air, freezing my movements. The cry came from the other side of the van.

"Don't anyone move from here!" warned the detective. Then he bolted away to check who screamed.

"Let's get outta here, daddy," said Headley.

"Huh?" I replied, "but the detective said we—"

"Oh, daddy...." Headley shook his head at my cluelessness.

"Okay, son. Let's roll." I took Fred's hand and waved for Mildead to follow.

"Hey, wait a minute," agent Walters spat out, "what about our deal? The sheet of paper."

"What sheet of paper?" I asked.

Fred pulled his hand away from my grip, took out a folded sheet of paper from his back pocket, and showed it to me.

Still, on his knees, Agent Walters stretched out an arm to receive the sheet of paper.

Headley took the folded sheet of paper from Fred and offered it to the CIA agent. Agent Walters reached for the paper, but Headley quickly snapped his hand back.

"Psyche...." Headley blurted. "We changed our minds."

Agent Walters had a look of confusion.

"Hey, we had a deal!"

"That was before we knew your true identity...agent Walters...of the C-I-A."

Agent Walters cleared his throat before he snapped, "That's right. I am a CIA agent. For national security reasons, I must have that piece of paper."

"Why? So you could keep hiding your secret dealings with the Chinese from our government? I don't think so. You are a traitor to this country, agent Walters. And because you're a criminal, my mom and my brother and I could eat your brain in four seconds flat. But, since you did help us get our daddy back, we'll allow you to live."

Agent Walters frowned.

"So, no sheet of paper?"

Fred wagged a finger at the agent, then gave him the Finger.

The sound of gunshots suddenly cracked off three times from the other side of the van.

"Daddy, Mommy, let's get outta here!" Headley cried out.

I snatched Fred's hand. "You don't have to tell me. Come on, boys! Come on, Mildead!"

As we were running away, I looked back to see if anyone was chasing us. But there was no one, and I was sure glad of that.

We tore off down Highland avenue, reaching Yucca street, where startled pedestrians danced out of our way. Up ahead, a few blocks away, several police cars with their sirens blazing, were headed toward us. I slowed my family down to a cruising pace, for I didn't want the cops to see us running away from the crime scene.

"Daddy, where are we going?" Headley asked.

"We're heading back to our car."

"You think that detective shot our aunties?"

I stopped walking and gestured to my family to hide behind a UPS truck. I then gazed back at the van that was now surrounded by police cars. Although Sodead and Toodead kidnapped me and wanted to eat my brain, I felt a tinge of worry for their well being.

"I don't know, son. Maybe they got away."

Headley bent his head back and spoke to his mother, "Mommy, do you think my aunties escaped?"

Mildead stayed silent for a brief moment, also staring back at the van. I had a feeling what she was doing—she was trying to hone in on the mental atmosphere surrounding her sisters. Zombies had an inherent connection with one another—, especially with undead siblings.

She soon turned to Headley and said, "yes. They escaped."

"Good," I said half-heartedly.

Headley heard my remark and asked, "why did you say 'good', daddy? Aunties Sodead and Toodead kidnapped you and were gonna eat your brain."

"I...I just want them to be okay. I can't help the way I feel, son. They are your family in a way, they're my family, too. Also, they didn't choose to be zombies—they do what they do—eat people's brains."

Fred walked up to me, and both of my sons gave me firm hugs.

"You're a good daddy," said Headley. Fred second Headley's remark with a thumbs up.

"Aww...thanks, you two," I uttered with welled up eyes. "That's the best thing anyone has ever said to me." With all the love I could muster, I hugged and kissed each of my beautiful sons. "Okay, come on. We gotta go."

We continued at a lively pace toward Hollywood boulevard, all the while looking back practically every five seconds to see if the cops were chasing us. We refrained from running, for we didn't want to seem suspicious or conspicuous. Although Fred and Headley stood out just a little bit since they were a kind of famous—they did have a hit commercial. We were already exhausted. These Los Angeles blocks seemed like a mile long. No wonder most people here used some type of transportation. The city is a vast landmass—too big for pedestrians, I thought.

We were finally on Hollywood boulevard, only a block away from our car. I checked my pocket for the car keys and was relieved when I grasped them in my hand.

Upon arriving only several yards from the Pacer, a worried Headley asked, "Daddy, do you think the cops are hiding out, waiting for us to show at our car?"

"Um...I don't think so. How could the cops know where our car—"

"Hands in the air!" detectives Lee and Vera shouted simultaneously. They had jumped out of their Crown Vic that was parked right behind my Pacer.

"Dammit!" I grunted.

Detective Lee's eyes seared at us. "I had told you three...uh, four... not to move away from the van. Now I'm pissed. Just give me a reason to shoot. All of you, get on your knees and put your hands behind your heads!"

I had to do something fast. If we go to jail, the detective might connect us to the death of Mr Dakimbo. There was no way he would believe that Mr Dakimbo's death had been an execution rather than a murder and that we were battling evil so that the world would be a better place. Maybe he would understand my family's unconventional, heroic deeds after all since his job was to uphold the law, I thought and hoped.

"Ex...excuse me, Mr Detective," I said in a nervous tone. "What if I told you that my family and I are enforcers of all that is good in mankind."

The detective returned a sarcastic nod. Then he gave me a look of exhaustion and spat, "Get the hell outta here. Now, shut up and get on your knees!"

"Hey, don't talk to my daddy like that!" Headley cut in.

"You shut up and get on your knees, too!" growled Detective Lee.

Headley breathed out a harrumph and shot back, "For your information, getting on my knees is highly unlikely given my permanent position, you bozo."

"Well, then tell your bottom half to get on his knees."

"You tell him. I'm not your slave," said Headley, who folded his arms and turned his head away from the detective.

Detective Lee took two hard steps toward Fred and Headley and shoved his gun inches away from them.

"Get on your freakin' knees!"

"Hey, point the gun at me! Not at my boys!" I rumbled.

The detective gladly accommodated me and aimed his gun at my head. "I'm not going to tell you again! Get on your damn knees!"

I ignored the detective and pointed behind him. "Look! It's the king of England!"

Detective Lee scoffed at my bluff while his partner turned her head listlessly.

All of a sudden, the woman detective dropped her gun on the ground. Then she started to shake.

With his gun still pointed at us, Detective Lee glanced at his partner with much concern and then raised his voice, "Vera, what the hell! What's wrong with you!" He then sidestepped over to her and put his hand on her shoulder, trying to stabilise the shaking.

"I don't know what...what's the matter with me, Phil," murmured the female detective who suddenly flopped in detective Lee's arms.

"Leslie!" Detective Lee carefully laid her down on the ground, then pointed his gun back at us and yelled, "Don't anyone move! And for the last time get on your freakin' knees!"

At once, my family and I dropped to our knees. Mildead was next to me and whispered something that I didn't hear.

"What?"

"She's turning," Mildead repeated.

"Turning? What do you mean, turning?"

"She's turning into a zombie."

I showed Mildead my I-don't-believe-you expression, looking like a squinting, wrinkled-up old man.

"No, she's not...."

Mildead returned a slight nod. Her silent affirmation only made her strange zombie remark more believable to me.

"Excuse me, Mr Detective! Excuse me!" I called out.

Detective Lee peeled his attention away from his partner who stopped shaking, and then he eyed me with disdain.

"What!"

"Um...I wouldn't be so close to that lady detective if I were you."

"What the hell is that supposed to mean?"

My eyes drifted to the Detective's female partner.

"Look!"

Detective Vera's olive-coloured skin was turning pale, and her once hazel eyes were now dilated and black as coal. Detective Lee was shocked and confused by his partner's sudden transformation. He then felt around the back of her head and neck and instantly pulled his hand away. Blood and tiny pieces of flesh saturated his fingertips. He moved her on her side and was stunned to see a four-inch, crater-like hole that was behind her neck.

Then his shock and confusion heightened when she smiled back at him.

"Hello, Phil. I'm hungry for your brain," said detective Vera whose voice was hoarse, not her usual light mousey tone.

"What? My brain?"

Detective Vera licked her lips and shot up, attempting to bite her partner on the neck, but Detective Lee managed to block her attack with his gun—she bit down on his 9mm Glock 19, shattering two of her front teeth.

"Leslie, what the hell are you doing?"

Detective Vera stretched her mouth open, releasing the gun, and she rolled away from detective Lee. She then lifted herself off the ground and stood up, wearing a wicked grin, and ogling detective Lee as though he was her favourite meal. She began to drift slowly toward him, desiring his flesh.

"I want to eat your brain. I want to eat your brain," Detective Vera chanted.

Detective Lee started to backpedal. "Leslie, what's happening to you?"

"Stay where you are, Phil. It will only take a few seconds."

Detective Lee kept moving backwards, away from his stalking partner. He reluctantly raised his gun and pointed it at her.

"Don't come any closer, Leslie. Or I'll...I'll."

"Or what, Phil. Shoot your partner. I'm hungry, Phil. I want to eat your brain. I want to..."

Detective Lee seemed helpless. He could not bring himself to shoot his zombie partner, so he continued to back off.

I turned to Mildead and said dryly, "I've certainly been there before."

Mildead looked back at me with that evil eye of hers. "Whatever."

My eyes lit up when the two detectives moved further away from us. Then my genius brain went to work, hiking up my IQ a couple of points to 78. I whispered to my family.

"Mildead. Boys, head over to the car. We're outta here."

Once we were outside of the Pacer, getting ready to open its doors, Detective Lee fired a shot into the air.

"Hey, get back here!" shouted the detective, who was still slowly backing away from his partner.

I shrugged my shoulders and said, "Sorry, Detective. We have an appointment with the...umm the mayor of Hollywood. Gotta go."

Detective Lee suddenly stopped and held his arms out. He oddly pointed the finger at me while he spoke nervously to his zombie partner.

"Leslie, what about that guy. His brain would taste much better than mine."

The zombie detective held her steps, then instantly turned my way. She grinned at me with greedy eyes and mummy-walked toward me.

"Dammit!" I began to fumble my car keys.

"Step back from the car, or I'll shoot!" yelled Detective Lee.

My hands shook as I finally stuck the key into the car door.

"We're late, Detective. The senator...I mean, the President, is waiting."

"If you open that door, you're dead!"

I certainly believed him, but I had to do something, so I pointed past the Detective and cried out.

"Look! It's the King of England!"

The first time I had tried my bluff against him, it hadn't worked. So I wasn't sure what possessed me to use the same bluff again. But by golly, it worked. He fell for my ruse and turned around, allowing me just enough time to unlock the door and get inside my car. I was more than surprised the man had turned around. I've always known that we lived in a world where some things cannot be explained, so I wasn't going to search for answers on why the Detective fell for my bluff the second time. Maybe it was a small miracle of God—a Devine invention, my mother had often said. As soon as I stuck the car key into the ignition, gunshots were fired, shattering the rear window.

"Hurry, Daddy!" Headley shouted.

"I'm tryin'. I'm tryin'," I said, as the engine was turning over.

The engine finally started, then as I put the car into drive, the zombie detective pounded on the driver-side window.

"I want to eat your brain," Detective Vera moaned.

"My little brain stays in my head, baby! Now outta my way!" I cut the steering wheel to the left and stepped on the gas pedal, then the Pacer squealed out of the parking space, leaving the two detectives in its wake.

"You did it, daddy!" praised Headley, who peeked out through the shattered rear window, as Fred stood on the back seat, showing the detectives his middle finger.

I glanced at the rearview mirror and asked, "Is Detective Lee getting into his car?"

"No, daddy. The lady is now chasing him."

"That's good news, son. Excellent news."

Fred turned away from the rear window and sat back down.

"Where are we heading to now, daddy?" Headley asked.

At that moment as I drove, I glanced up at the smoggy Los Angeles sky and replied.

"To a land where the innocent need our help to fight the darkness. To a land where evil lurks, infecting all that is good."

Headley smiled, "Vegas?"

"That's right, son. Vegas, baby."

"Cool!"

As my little zombie family and I headed east toward the desert in our 1978 Pacer, we were once again singing our favorite song.

"♪... Oh, you pretty chitty bang bang, chitty chitty bang bang, we love you. And our pretty chitty bang bang loves us too. High, low, anywhere we go on chitty chitty we depend. Bang bang chitty chitty bang bang, our fine four fendered friend. Bang bang chitty chitty bang, our fine four fendered friend!♪"

The End